Explosive Orders

Charles Joynson

Chapter 1

Ivan James closed the door and hung his cap on a hook. Sitting heavily on the hall chair he pulled off his muddy boots and pushed them to one side. His wet barber he hung below the cap. The house was still warm, thanks to the Aga in the kitchen. He went through, filled the kettle and put it on the hob. A good mug of tea was the best way to warm up after a cold day. This April was particularly cold, with freezing winds from the north and snow flurries in the early mornings, leaving the fields frosty white at first light.

All told however, it had been a good day; he'd sold four ewes and some lambs at Hatherley market and was reasonably happy with the price they'd fetched. He was pleased that lamb prices had risen of late and the farm had a chance of paying its way again.

The farm was an old one, Greenly Barton, had stood looking down on a slow lazy bend in the river Torrage since the 13th century when it had been built as a cattle shed. It had been added to by successive generations of farmers and had grown into a very nice little farm, with 185 acres of land. 35 of which were down on the flood plain, excellent grazing for Ivan's beloved Red Devon cattle. The rest was mainly on the higher ground, and here he had fields of kale and potatoes.

Having finished his tea, he rose from the kitchen table, leaving the cup and pot for Mrs. Scibble to wash when she came 'to do' on Friday. He went through to the old dining room and taking the day's profits from his wallet he stuck it into a tin in the gun cupboard.

Yes, it had been a good day, and a glass of whisky was called for. That had been a present from one of his nephews, though he'd forgotten which one, with ice but not too much water. Hatherley Market was good in the cold months as the weather kept the bloody tourists away. Dammed women in high heels goose stepping over sheepshit, and getting in the way of the business of the day, and with malcontented children who would rather have been on the beach.

Once or twice Ivan had been tempted to drive the sheep at them, or obligingly open a gate when he knew thick mud lay beyond.

The new roads they were building had brought hordes of tourists into what had been previously deepest Devon, where everybody knew everybody else, as well as quite probably their parents, nephews and cousins. Into this close quiet world had come hordes of tourists on their holidays and then worst of all, wanted to stay. Retired policemen form Bristol, pub landlords from Brixton, even widows from Cheltenham. As far as Ivan was concerned, if he didn't go in to Bristol, London or Cheltenham, in fact he'd never been to Bristol, London or Cheltenham, and had no intention of ever doing so, then these boldly tourists should return the favor and bugger off back to where they came from.

Many of the old villages had been spoiled, Somleigh, the nearest, had doubled in size, with estates of brick built houses full of incomers with foul habits, bad manners and accents which made some of them sound as if they were gargling with bloody marbles.

There were advantages in the different accents, friends had told Ivan, as you can use some lovely old Devon insults, and they think you're complimenting them on something or other.

He closed the gun cupboard, turned the light off and shut the door. Always had been a cold room, that dining room, one day he would do something about it. But then there were so many things which needed doing to the old house. The thatch had gone at one end and the roof had come in on him during a particularly heavy storm one night three years before, leaving him cold, wet and covered with straw and plaster right in the middle of an excellent dream about the landlady of the Royal Oak.

He'd gone off her a bit after that.

When he was a boy his father had told him that the farm would set him up for life. "A very good little place, you look after it and it will look after you," he told his son, or on other occasions, "you reap what you sow son."

What his dear departed father hadn't told him were his regular trips to the pheasant shooting at Bovey Tracey had in fact been jaunts to the racing at Exeter. When the old boy had finally decided to turn his boots skyward and kick the bucket, he'd left his son with massive racing debts and shattered dreams. And then there'd been the death duties, bloody crippling in the 1950s, and half the land had had to go to pay them. For a long time he'd worked like hell on the farm, or at least until after his wife had died.

He went through into the sitting room, turned on the TV and poured himself the promised whisky. He fetched ice from the fridge in the kitchen and slumped down into his father's big ass chair. The bottom had fallen out years ago, but he'd replaced it with extra layers of cushions and nailed boards. Like everything else it was old and had certainly seen better days. The TV was still black and white and he'd never had one of the new-fangled remote machines, but preferred instead to use a billiard cue to change channels. Focusing on the TV for a moment he noticed that what should have been North Devon News, was on about some bloody awful heavy metal band called Cordaxe, he reached for the cue and changed the channel, he could do without that kind of rubbish.

He finished his whisky, put the glass on the coffin stool by his side, and let his chin slip down onto his chest and dozed. When he woke it was past seven, and he decided to wander up to the pub in the village and have a pint or two of Ferrets with some friends.

He was a great fan of Ferrets Ale, brewed in South Moxton from, some said real ferrets, but most genuine Devonians he knew swore by the stuff. Those who drank it never seemed to catch colds or flu, and seemed a pretty tough lot. Dr Hughes, the local GP would have said that North Devon's farming folk were just a remarkably hardy bunch, and rarely came to see him unless they had at the very least lost a finger or stepped on an unexploded incendiary. There were still a few of these about, dropped by German bombers that had missed Exeter, and wanted to get home without the extra weight.

But most North Devon people would have retorted that when they did go aboard, meaning Somerset, and couldn't get Ferrets, then they came down with all manner of ailments from gout to the pox.

Putting the boots and Barbour back on again, he made his way out to the old stable where he'd left the van.

The stable was an old Nissan hut leftover from the first war. It had been used as a stable in his father's day, however the front of it was now used as a garage and the back had been walled off to form a convenient kennel. This is where he kept a cross collie sheepdog called Pitch. She was a very good sheepdog, excellent on the hills and at a distance bringing in the sheep on a cold winter's day. She had terrific hearing, and could pick up his whistles at least a mile away. But for some unknown reason Pitch had a thing about colours and would attack anything red with terrific fury.

As such he kept the animal well secured and only took her out with the sheep or elsewise on a strong chain. Pitch raised her head and watched him as he refilled her water bowl.

She made no move to rise, as - unknown to Ivan - while he'd been in the market, and had thought her well secured in the van, a fire engine had parked a little too close for comfort. It was there to give a display to the local children. In fact Pitch couldn't have risen if she'd wanted to, as doing a very passable impression of a rabid banshee for four hours had completely exhausted the animal.

He walked towards the village, having decided that the ground was too wet for the bicycle and he could do with the fresh air. In the summer it was a nice little ride up to the village, but at this time of year it was just too muddy. The light was gradually fading as the sun sank behind the hills in the West, and on the other side of the valley he could hear an owl hooting.

The countryside at this time of year was very pretty, daffodils were flowering in the hedgerows, and snowdrops were just finishing. Catkins were hanging from the hazel branches and the pollen was drifting smoke-like across the lanes.

Darkness on the other hand reminded him that Devon had the last vestige of the wild forests that once covered the whole of England. There were still wild things in the woods around Devon. Some years before he'd noticed large paw prints in the mud one winter's day while he was closing a woodland gate. They were too big for a domestic cat, and certainly not a dog. Mind you, he'd kept that one quiet. Otherwise you could have loads of journalists or worse wandering around your farm, frightening the sheep, leaving gates open, damaging crops and so on.

So he'd taken to searching the open fields for more tracks with his gun on his arm, as even an idiot knows big cats can best be seen in open country where you

can see them before they see you. But he'd never seen anything more.
The first part of the walk was on a mud track, which had once been the main
entrance to the farm, now only used occasionally to get to the fields down by
the river, and by sheep sheltering from the rain. After ten minutes he left this
green lane, passed the old car, covered by years of accumulated moss, and
joined the road up to the village, passing Archie's house on route. The car had
been Archie's, but when it had given up the ghost some years before he'd left it
where it had fallen so to speak. The house lights were off and only the presence
of the newer - but seemingly equally ancient Morris indicated that Archie was
near at hand. Archie farmed a few acres bordering the stream leading down to
the Torrage, and had a few sheep, which eked a meager living out of the rough
grass that grew along its banks. Archie on occasion would complain that the
bloody things had got out again; Ivan thought that it was Archie's own fault as
he rarely bothered to repair his gates or fences. Well-meaning passers-by would
then open a convenient gate and usher the sheep into the nearest field.
Although Archie complained about this, it did provide him with free grazing
until the owner of the field spotted the sheep and informed Archie of the
trespass, usually with a demand for repatriation.
Archie was probably in his middle seventies, but it was difficult to say with
certainty, as he looked so unkempt. He had a broad Devon accent, and was well
known for his local knowledge. A couple of years before he'd been recorded
telling stories for a historical archive that was being built up, and had even been
allowed to sing some local folk songs.
Archie, was also well known for his poaching activities, as he'd been at one time
at any rate the best poacher in North Devon, and had been seen once or twice
wearing a tie in Torrington after having made his apologies to the magistrate.
Archie knew the District from the underside, undersides of hedges, banks,
woods and other sources of game. He had spent many a night under a hedge
waiting for a rabbit or pheasant, but seldom talked about it. He claimed he was
now too old and arthritic for such activities and his only contact with hedges
was on summer evenings on his way back from the pub after too many pints of
Ferrets.
Once or twice Ivan had received a trout in return for not looking too closely
when he saw Archie doing a bit of covert fishing. Particularly as the fishing
below the farm belonged to a Brigadier-General from Bideford who had would
have blown a gasket if he'd known Archie was helping himself to his fish.
He bent his back and forced himself up the hill to the village. It is dark now and
only the village lights showed ahead, a comforting orange in the darkness. The
sky was heavy with overhanging cloud, which warned of rain, but he felt warm
with the effort and took little notice.
There were three pubs in the village, the first the Union was the smart one full
of tourists eating garlic bread and prawns. It had originally been used by the
more affluent among the tradesmen of the district, and even the squire and his

family had been seen there in the past. It was now part of a chain and offered standardized microwaved mush to the traffic passing on route from Bideford to Exeter. The second was the George, which catered for the newer residents of the village. He would not be seen dead in there, not that he would have understood the accents used anyway. It had jukeboxes, and snooker, and other inventions of the devil, as the Vicar might have said.

He turned right at the village cross and headed for the Royal Oak, the smallest of the three, which was frequented by farmers and others who had true blue Devon blood in their veins. The Royal Oak was not to the liking of the newer residents of the village. There were no jukeboxes, flashing lights or loud music, sawdust had only recently disappeared from the floor, the walls are paneled, and hung with the heads and tails of long dead sporting trophies. Neither were they likely to see coaches full of tourists asking for French cooking nor ice creams, in fact food was limited to pork scratchings and crisps, and only the more conventional flavors at that. No bloody prawn cocktail at the Royal Oak thank God, thought Ivan.

Sometimes he wished the food was a bit better, but he would rather have had the meager snacks that Royal Oak served up than the crowds of ghastly tourists filling the bar and shouting at each other.

He pushed the paneled door open and walked into the bar. Pipe smoke, the smell of warm beer and gentle conversation greeted him like an old friend. He made his way to the bar and ordered a pint of ferrets, and then sought out the table near the open fire under the chimneybreast. Archie was already there, pipe in mouth and a pint of Ferrets in front of him.

The greeted each other and Ivan drew up a chair.

Archie sucked on his pipe and a cloud of sweet-smelling smoke surrounded his aged head.

They discussed Ivan's day at Hatherley market.

Archie asked about the sheep and lamb prices, and seemed pleased to hear that they were rising at last.

"It will be fine if we didn't have to put up with all these ruddy tourists" complained Ivan.

"They're not bliddy toorsts, and well you know it," retorted Archie, "just cos they don't wear wellies, speak Devon and have a good covering of mud, it don mean that they are a torist. Just cos they has been living here less 50 year, and don belong tut wellie and Barbour brigade, don mean there grackles, I mean some of them new farmers don't even farm sheep no more, and a load of them dress funny anyway.

There's even farmers over Bristow way that farm llamas, and there's farmers all-over farming ostriches, the world's changing Ivan and there is nothing you or I can do 'bout it."

Ivan took another mouthful of beer and shook his head. "I know the world's changing Archie, I just don't see why we should just lie back and let it change -

without at least of giving it a run for its money."

Archie tapped his pipe out in the ashtray and started to refill it.

"That lot up the George will end up being the next generation that the world thinks are pure Devon folk, but then in 50 year who will care?"

"Over my dead bloody body," responded Ivan.

"Well, there tiz and caint be no tizzer!"

They sat in silence for some time, contemplating their beer and enjoying the warmth and conviviality of the pub. Occasionally the door opened and a thickly coated figure would appear out of the cold night. At the bar two young men in jackets were discussing the merits of various beers with the barmaid. They were locals all right, but worked in Exeter, as many of the latest generation had difficulty finding work on the land and had to resort to working as salesmen, building society managers or clerks in offices.

Ivan thought this resorted to selling their souls to the devil, life in a suit seemed to him worse than his few years in uniform.

Later the door flew open and Charlie appeared.

Charlie was a thinning man in his early sixties. He sported a faded green hat, emblazoned with the word "Uniright," which had something to do with his career in the motorway building business. Charlie was well known for his over developed sense of humor, and was grinning broadly as he approached.

He was known for his practical jokes, as at one time he'd developed quite a reputation for phoning people up with a piece of cheese in his mouth and telling them some great story. One of his best had been telling them that he was from the water board, and that as their water was to be cut off for 24 hours, they would be well advised to fill any spare containers. Sometimes he waited twenty minutes to allow them to fill all the storage jars and cooking pots, and start filling the bath, before phoning back to give the game away, but with people he didn't like so much, he never phoned back at all.

"Evening to you both," he grinned,

"Evening Charlie" they replied.

Charlie was almost always in a good mood, but today he was positively ebullient. In fact he was in an extremely good mood. He started by offering to buy a round, which was quickly accepted and three fresh pints of Ferrets appeared on the table. Charlie straddled a stool next to the fire and grinned broadly at Archie and Ivan.

They knew something was up, but also suspected that he might bore them to tears with whatever it was, or worse it could be another leg pull. As pleased as they were with the seldom offered round of drinks, they remained silent in an effort to delay or prevent Charlie talking them both to death.

"Have you heard? I've had some good news," Charlie started, however when he realized no response was to be forthcoming he continued, "You know I was after that job, you know, we saw it in the morning news, the one down at Mill House with the new people, well I got it! I just went straight down there and asked, just knocked on the door, and this feller came out and I said I wanted the work, and he said, yes, no problem, whatever, start on Monday.

Didn't think it would be that easy, I just knocked on the door, I thought that at least there might be some sort of interview or something, but he just said, 'Start on Monday!'

There is normally an interview isn't there, I mean when I got the job at the garage I had to do all sorts of stuff, forms, tests and stuff, but he just said 'Start on Monday'.

Do you think I should have turned him down?

I mean to get a job so easily; it's not natural somehow, like you would think there was something wrong with the job."

Archie, who was somewhat deaf, probably due to his shotguns, had only heard part of all this due to the laughter coming from the bar. Gripping his pipe firmly between his teeth he asked "Monday, what's with Monday?"

Oh hell, thought Ivan, that's done it, we'll never shut him up now.

Charlie leant towards Archie conspiratorially, "You know after I left the garage, I was after something, a little less strenuous, you know how they worked me there, well I heard that that the new people were after a gardener, and I thought perfect, a little bit of light work and a little extra cash. Perfect. I couldn't ask for more, and he just said 'start on a Monday'. I couldn't believe my luck."

"They probly need a sacrifichal victim," Ivan threw in.

"Don't be stupid," snapped Charlie "I'm not walking in with my eyes closed, but a job's a job. If they try anything I'll walk straight out, don't you worry about me."

"Probably daft people down from London, maize as a brush," interjected Ivan, keen to keep Charlie off balance. "You never can tell with people that come down here, sometimes they're trying to get away from something or up to something not quite proper. You'd better keep your eyes peeled Charlie, you never know."

Joanna, collecting empties with a tray, overheard them and commented. "I hear they're a pop group." But before they could reply she had returned to the bar.

"Bliddy awful," commented Archie.

"There was bloke from over Appledore way," Ivan continued "who used to do a strange dance on one of the jetties after breakfast each day, but he had no idea he was doing it. Been on LSD while in America or something. And the chap in Witheridge who explained why he'd beaten his wife up by saying he thought she was a big brown bear. He was on something. Oh yes, and there was a maid over Chulmleigh way that used to run everywhere. She wasn't a keep-fit fanatic or anything like that; she was in her fifties, and not some young thing. When she went to the shops she would run there, run around the shelves with her basket, run on the spot while she paid, and then she would run home with her shopping bags in her hands. Sometimes when people drove past they would see her jogging on the spot and waiting for a bus."

7

"I heard bout some folk," said Archie "a few years backalong, had come down from upcuntree, down near Bovey Tracey I think it were and they had a thing about not washing, and walked on tissues and towels and that. They were into drinking each other's urine, in some sort of commune.
So you watch yourself, and if they offer you anything to drink boy, smell it first!"
"Oh buggar off!" said Charlie.

Chapter 2

The following afternoon Archie decided that he would work the hedges to the east of Mill House. It was a good one for rabbits and it might also give him a chance to have a look at the new occupants. Collecting a bag of snares from his lean-to, he glanced momentarily at the gin traps rusting in an ammunition box at the back and made his way across the bridge and up the hill.
He remembered as a child his father had shown him how to net rabbits, it had been a great skill and entailed spreading the net between the field where they were eating and the hedge with their burrows under it. The best they had done was thirty-six rabbits in a single night. But when he came back after the war the net had vanished, and he couldn't get another one. After that he'd had to use gin traps but they were cruel, sometimes leaving just a leg in the trap and were banned in the end any way. Now snares were the only option, unless of course he took a gun, however he preferred to be away from houses for that, otherwise people started coming out to find out what was up.
He opened the gate and let himself into the field, the corn was growing well and was standing green and formed luxuriant tablecloth across the field. On the side nearest Mill House there was considerable damage to the crop, as there was a well-used warren there. It had probably been there for hundreds of years.
Would be absolutely ideal for a net, but snares would do. The thumping beat of pop music floated across the field toward him from the vicinity of Mill House, loud and jarring in the peace of the countryside. He made his way along the hedge pushing the stakes in beside commonly used runways, remembering that he would have to check them early the next morning, before the fox got to them.
After he'd pushed all the stakes well into the ground, and draped the wire nooses over slender stems of grass, he crept through the hedge and made his way on all fours into a rhododendron bush that bordered the Lawn of Mill House.
The house massive and solid as it was, was not as old as it appeared. It had originally been a water mill, and the leat or water channel that used to feed the water wheel were still under the lawn somewhere. The old mill pool which had once fed the great wheel was now an ornamental fish pond, the wheel of course

8

was long gone and the drop had been landscaped, so that there was no longer any evidence of the building's previous function.

At some point in the 19th century, the mill had been enlarged, by a fossil collector of all people who had moved to the area, and had been mining fossils from the cliff behind the house. Another three floors had been built above the existing building, and the old mill itself had been converted into cellars beneath the new house. The gardens had been landscaped, and only the slightest of dips in the lawns indicated that the building had been constructed on a stream.

The house itself backed onto the old quarry, but there was little evidence of that now, the centuries had allowed vegetation to completely swamp the rock face. The main entrance on his right faced the parking area with the old stables beyond it flanking the drive.

He remembered his father telling him that he'd been up to the house once. After the Great War, the old man had made saddles and horse harnesses, but as horses disappeared from the countryside and were replaced by tractors, he'd started working as a carpenter and joiner. He had been called up to the house to repair a game larder that was completely rotten, and had had to smash the old one up to get it out. When he'd finished, he said that instead of the wall that he'd expected, he'd found a narrow cleft in the living rock - going straight into the hillside. The old man had had a job to do, and no time for exploring caves, so had got on with repairing the larder. But he said from what he saw it might have gone right through that hill and out the other side.

There seemed to be a party going on in the house, the French windows were open and people were coming and going between the house and the patio. The noise was deafening even from where he squatted in the dark of the bush. Someone was fooling around throwing things at the statues on the grass, Archie wasn't sure what was that was being thrown, but from the sound, thought it might have been wine glasses. A man came out through the French windows, climbed over the stone balustrade and proceeded to urinate into the ornamental fishpond. No one on the patio took the slightest notice.

Archie, unimpressed by the new residents, retraced his steps back through the hedge and made his way homeward. He didn't think it would matter if did use a gun, that lot were too drunk to take any notice anyway.

As he climbed back over the gate into the lane, he could still hear the infernal din emanating from Mill House and disturbing the peace of the afternoon. If they can't keep a bit quieter he thought to himself, they ought to have stayed in London or wherever it was they had come from.

Now country noises, they were a different matter. The hunt kennels could get a bit noisy at times, so could point to point, and banger racing on a Saturday afternoon, and farmers calling their cattle in for milking and the church bells of course. But they were country noises, and people knowing they were country noises ignored them because they were county noises. But the sounds coming from Mill house were not country noises and had no place in the country as far as he was concerned.

Anyway, he wasn't sure Charlie was going to enjoy working there.

On the Monday morning Charlie made his way down the rhododendron fringed drive just before 9 o'clock. He was somewhat apprehensive, and remembered when he'd started the job in the garage, as he'd been just as nervous that time. However he recalled that he'd got into the job and quickly became more confident.

At the front of the House many cars were parked, some on the drive and others on the grass.

He was impressed with these, lots of Jaguars, some Mercedes, even a couple of Ferraris.

He noticed that the drive itself that crunched under his feet was not composed of gravel but of tiny seashells. Lichen stained statues observed his progress from the lawn, and he wondered what they thought about his new employers.

His made he made his way up to the porch and the great oak door, and finding no bell, struck the heavy iron doorknocker against the wood. The echo seemed to reverberate through the building. He could hear no activity from within and wondered if he was to be ignored. After some minutes he repeated the action and again listened to the echo as it echoed through the building. Eventually he heard faint footfalls from somewhere distant within, and after some minutes the door opened and a man appeared. He seemed to be in his early fifties and wore an immaculate suit and red bow tie, but most noticeable of all was that his hair seemed to have been permed, appearing thick and swept-back, more fitting a man in his twenties. He wondered if this was the butler and if the hair might be a wig.

He explained why he was there and the man nodded and seemed to accept his explanation.

"Yes, I've been expecting you, you're late!"

Charlie knew he wasn't, but thought it better not to disagree.

The man came through the door and guided Charlie back onto the driveway.

"There are a number of things you will need to understand. Firstly you will not enter the house on any occasion. You will limit your activities to the gardens and the outbuildings. You will not, I repeat not, attempt to enter or even look into the house on any pretext or excuse. Do you understand?"

"Um, yes of course, if that's what you want," stammered Charlie.

"If there is anything you need you will contact me, and will not annoy any of the guests or residents in the House. My name is Mr. Fox," and he gave Charlie a business card.

Charlie looked down at the gold lined card as the instructions continued.

"You will find tools and equipment in the outhouses behind the house; you will not make any noise at all before 2 o'clock in the afternoon. That specifically means mowing lawns, and you must finish mowing by 6 o'clock each evening."

"You will be paid at the end of each month with a cheque, which will be sent to

your home, so I will need personal details as soon as you can provide them."
Charlie reached into an inside pocket and produced a P45 which had been given
to him by the garage.
"Good."
Richard Fox looked at the P45, and then seemed to forget Charlie's existence.
He turned, made his way back into the house and closed the door behind him.
Charlie was left feeling rather bemused; it hadn't been like this when he'd started
work at the garage. He turned and made his way around the side of the house to
the old coaching stables. Opening one door at a time he eventually found a
room full of mowing and gardening equipment. On the walls, wooden racks
hung with tools, all well organized and easy to reach. The back of the room was
cluttered with rolls of chicken wire, fencing posts and more shelving.
He found the mover, mounted on wood blocks and located an oil can. It was
too wet yet for mowing, but the lawns would need a mow as soon as it dried out
a little. Bending over the old machine he set to work on the engine. It didn't
look as if it had been used since old Hedon had died, and a couple of years of
disuse had allowed it to rust up somewhat.
It took until lunchtime to get it going again, but eventually he succeeded, and sat
back satisfied to eat his sandwiches. He pulled the business card from his pocket
and studied it, 'Richard Fox, Business Manager,' it said with black and gold
lettering. Charlie wondered what a business manager was, perhaps a new term
for a butler and put the card back into his pocket.
Later he took a tour of the grounds, identifying which plants and trees would
need thinning or removing. It was a good garden and he very much looked
forward to working in it, although it looked as though it might be a thankless
task. But the consolation was that he appeared to have a free hand, and aside of
digging up the lawn, could do anything he wanted. Glancing up at the house
across the lawns he noticed a couple in one of the upper bedroom windows,
they were dancing to some unheard beat, completely naked. No sense of dignity
at all, he thought as he made his way back to the stables.
You wouldn't catch Maureen and me dancing naked in front of our bedroom
window, he thought as he opened the door. However there had been that time
after when they had got themselves caught skinny dipping in a Warwickshire
lake, but that had been a long time ago, and now Maureen was frightening
enough with her clothes on. Naked she might give some poor old boy, passing
by innocently in the road, a heart attack.
Inside the house Richard Fox walked across the hall to the study with the P45
clutched in his hand. He put it into an envelope, scribbled a quick note, and
stuck a label addressing it to his accountant in Southend on Sea. He'd run a
business there, before becoming the band's business manager. Phobia City it
had been called, a warehouse full of snakes, spiders and rats. If only his partner
had done what he was supposed to do. A bloody crook, who had spent his time
in the casino when he was supposed to be looking after the animals. In the end

the animals had been the business's downfall, the snakes had bitten the customers, the spiders had died and the rats had escaped.

It had finally been closed by health and safety on health grounds, mainly they said because the rats had moved into the local fast food restaurants, which complained, saying that one of the largest of the rats had fallen into the boiling oil in a local fish and chip shop and had been inadvertently served to a Blues supporter with his chips.

Later a number of bed and breakfast establishments objected as well, saying their clients were finding rats in their rooms. Richard hadn't believed either story, suspecting that the council had put the complainants up to it.

Anyway malicious rumors were normally his territory, like the time he'd told the Mayor – who couldn't keep his mouth shut for more than five minutes at a time – that it was a great secret, but that the health inspectors had found salmonella in the cockles. Within a week the sea food restaurants had lost most of their custom, and they had got the site for the Phobia City three months later for next to nothing.

It had been fortuitous that a cousin's friend was looking for a manager for his band, and all the rest, Cordaxe and all, was history. All that had been four years ago, and the band had now had three number ones, and was in the charts in the UK and the US, with tours arranged, record deals, spin-offs, and other money-making schemes. If only they were a little more generous with money, all he wanted was a fair share; however there were always other ways. He had come in on a salary rather than a profit share, and the band had made him stick to it rather than treating him as a partner and giving him a percentage share of the increasing profits. OK they had put his salary up, but that was a joke in itself, when they were earning millions, all they were willing to give him was a tiny fraction of what he was helping them to make.

Mill House had been the home of the local squire and had been owned by an old man called Brooke. He had died a couple of years before, and a caretaker had been looking after the place. Apparently Brooke had made it his life's work to spend the family fortune, and had squandered vast sums on trips into the interior of South America during the 1950s. Looking for a giant sloth or something, he'd been told. He had returned from the trip with jaguars, panthers, parrots and the skins of numerous endangered species. Eventually the big cats had developed a taste for the local dogs and the fingers of anyone foolish enough to try to feed them. So the old man, with changes in the law in mind presumably, had phoned around the local zoos, but when he was told no one wanted them, and that oversupply had created a buyer's market, he had transferred them to their traveling cages and released them on the moors, where they proceeded to decimate the local sheep population.

Eventually the old man had died at the age of 85, but the estate could not be sold until the heirs were found and the will was proved.

The brief they had given to their agent had been to find somewhere secluded but comfortable for the group. They have looked at various places around Britain after the damned press had made their lives such a misery that they seriously considered either moving abroad, or disbanding the group and going their separate ways. They'd had a place in London for some years now, but with the press and photographers continually besieging it, it was almost impossible to use. So they had had to hire places on short-term lets, but the stress and hassle of it all was getting to them.

It was only after a chance remark by a young secretary working for the record label that he'd found Mill House. He had overheard her talking with a receptionist while he was waiting for a meeting, she had said that she had been to visit an aunt of hers in Devon, but had had great difficulty finding the place. When she had finally found the place, it turned out that her aunt had been care-taking and cleaning the old house.

After that he'd had a word with the agent and within a week they had started negotiating for a purchase. It was absolutely ideal, isolated, with a sparse local population, difficult to find, in fact so much so, that a couple of weeks before he'd had to drive to Tiverton to lead the decorators vans in convoy to the house.

The place had been a total mess when they had first arrived, the main reception area inside the porch had been a trophy room, with the moth addled heads and skins of long-dead animals lining the walls. A very large stuffed grizzly stood at the base of the stairs, claws raised and seeming ready to attack unwary guests! From the trophy room doors led through into dining and drawing rooms, each well lit and with plenty of space. They had bought the place contents and all, and had sold most of the stuff in a local sale. The stuffed grizzly had had to remain, as was too large to go through the doors. God only knew how they had got it into the house in the first place.

The builders had had to pretty much strip the place and redecorate everything, but it was at last beginning to look reasonable. They had had some friends down over the weekend, and had had a good time despite the ladders and scaffolding. It turned out that they had bought more than just a house, lots of land, buildings, a couple of farms, and some businesses and other things. He had his ideas about what do with parts of it, but was keen to hang on to the land because it gave them seclusion and privacy, the farms could be sold off, and they had agreed in principle that he could try and run the businesses as going concerns. As the group had given him a free hand with them, it occurred to him that he might find a way to supplement his paltry salary, but realized that he would need to exercise some degree of discretion with that one.

Chapter 3

The Reverend Peter Lethbridge the Vicar of Somleigh, Worleigh and Dowford sat in his study in Somleigh Vicarage and try to think of a topic for his sermon the following Sunday.

He had heard the news from his parishioners and knew that they had new residents in the village, and whoever they were and whatever they were like, they could make a great deal of difference to the lives of his congregation. For good or for evil he thought.

However, what little he knew of the lives of rock musicians and particularly heavy metal musicians, scant though it was, suggested that they would not bring a positive influence to bear on the morals of the local population. However he believed that if he preached a sermon against the sins of sex, drugs and rock'n'roll, although his meager congregation on Sunday might both agree and approve of his thoughts, it might upset the incoming residents and create a stereotype that might be hard to overcome.

Perhaps a sermon on good neighborliness might be more appropriate, after all these rock musician chappies might be thoroughly nice, unlikely but possible. It was he thought more likely they were the spawn of Satan, but he believed very strongly that they should not make hasty judgments without getting to know them first.

The Reverend Lethbridge was a man of close on 70, an experienced parish priest of great understanding. He came from an old Devon family with its roots in the area as far back as the Conquest. He knew a great deal of the area's history and even more about its people, having ministered to them for almost 42 years, he was fairly close to attaining the parish record.

Being a Devon man, he'd chosen to stay in the area he loved rather than be promoted and sent elsewhere, and for him this was no sacrifice. He had found a willing friend in the Bishop who had understood his love of the district.

Through his window the Vicar saw the lights of a van passing in the lane below. Probably Ivan James on his way home from the pub. The Vicar's mind moved to the subject of the local beverage, Ferrets Ale, as some of his local parishioners were rather too keen to on the stuff, even going so far as to use it for making biscuits and cakes. He didn't mind an occasional tipple himself and was very fond of a good glass of Malt whisky, but the way they drank Ferrets, anyone would think that they were worried it might run out. Some of them even claimed it was a cure for all known ills. Even Mrs. Weaver who decorated the church and was a leading light in the local Women's Institute, used the stuff in her cooking, and allegedly made wart cures from it.

But then he thought, that living in this modern world, it all seemed rather innocuous, his worrying about beer when some of his colleagues from the cities had far greater problems with drugs. So as long as they didn't find a way to inject Ferrets, it was just a minor local issue.

It was getting late and so he quickly jotted some ideas down for his sermon, and went up to his bed.

On the Sunday, after Holy Communion, he fell into conversation with two local worthies, and promised to go down to Mill House and greet the new owners. This was something he'd meant to do anyway, but Col Smyth demanded that he, "Go over to the place and find out what the buggers are up to," and ominously, "before its too late."

He had made a promise and would have seen it through that afternoon. However, he was sidetracked by a sick parishioner and had to plan the visit for the Monday.

On his way home he passed Ivan riding his gray mare, no sign of hounds or hunt, but Ivan gave him a cheery wave.

He liked Ivan; he recognized that he was one of God's own creations, very much an eccentric, being almost bald, with bright red ears which stuck out on each side of his head like sails, quite a short and dumpy little man. Ivan did come to Church occasionally and had even helped with some of the charity events trying to keep Somleigh Church in one piece. He was certainly a member of Christ's family, but the stories around him did lead the Vicar to be somewhat cautious in his dealings with Ivan.

He remembered one cold winter's day when the Gaunts at Upper Hilltop Farm, across the river from Ivan's place, had noticed smoke coming from Greenly Barton, great clouds of it through both doors and windows. The fire brigade were duly called and arrived only after some 20 minutes to find the house still intact but with smoke billowing from every crack and crevice.

They started to put on her their breathing apparatus, but before they could get to work on the fire, they were attacked by Ivan's dog, which laid siege to them, in and on the engine. Only when they had managed to give it a good drenching with a high pressure hose had it retreated, and had stood snarling at them from the far end of the farmyard.

The firemen then entered the house to find the source of the blaze, and going into the drawing room had found Ivan apparently completely unconcerned, reading a newspaper and wearing a World War II gas mask. Later, when the chimney had been put out, he was asked for an explanation and simply said that he'd been short of firewood, and thought he would try to burn dried cow muck, as he'd plenty of that, and he'd heard that was what they did in India!

On the Monday, shortly after 3pm in the afternoon, the Vicar drove his shooting-brake car up the old drive to Mill House. As he passed through the thick rhododendron jungle fringing the drive, he wondered what his reception was to be like. Coming around the bend at the end he found himself in front of house. Yes it was still a very nice house, even if it had been empty for a few years. Scaffolding was piled near the entrance, warning the Vicar that building work was taking place. He parked in a spare space, and made his way nervously towards the main entrance, where a gang of burly men were unloading a delivery van. He remembered wedding receptions there, many years ago now, when he was still a young man. They had been marvelous sumptuous affairs, the bride and groom arriving from the Church in a coach and six, guests in tail coats and beautiful dresses, marvelous food, the bridal couple cutting the cake with a Napoleonic sword. It all seemed a very long time ago.

Things had been different in those days of course. The Brooke family had been real gentry, with teams of servants at every door, footmen, butlers and maids. The village of course had been their private fiefdom, and their word was law. Luckily when he'd taken on the parish, Squire Brook had approved of him. Otherwise he might have ended up priest in some inner city somewhere.

The door was open, so he walked through, sidestepping workmen carrying boxes into the house. It was certainly a shock to see the house in its present stripped condition, as he remembered it the way it had been all those years before. Gone were the heads and skins of long-dead animals from all over the world, gone were all the cabinets of soft paste China that squire Brooke had made it his life's work to collect. Gone were all the glowering Ancestors, staring disapprovingly down from their gilded frames. He did notice that the old grizzly was still there, covered with a dustsheet. It had probably been too large to get through the door, and who would want such a monster anyway. A sad end to an era he thought.

In the drawing room he found more gangs of men doing things with wood and paint. A tall man in the center of the room with his back to the Vicar looked like a foreman, so the Vicar went across, stepping carefully over toolboxes to reach him.

"Good afternoon," he said as an introduction,

The man turned, and gave the Vicar a rather surprised look. He appeared to be about 50, tall, but prematurely aged, with a face lined by deep cracks that looked unnatural on anyone younger than 70 years old. His hair was brown, but rather dirty and knotted, and his eyes seemed to have some difficulty in focusing.

"Oh, hi," he replied in, what the Vicar took to be an American accent, "can I help you?"

The Vicar introduced himself, and asked if he could be introduced to the new owners of the House.

"Yes, that's me, at least part owner anyway," explained the man.

"Oh, right, I just wanted to be the first to welcome you to the parish and to extend the hand of friendship from the local population and the Church."

While he was saying this, the man began hitting his right ear with the ball of his right hand, and seemed to have some difficulty in focusing.

"Sorry, could you say that again?" he asked with furrowed brow.

The Vicar repeated himself.

"OK, thanks," the man replied.

"So, are you the new master?" the Vicar sought to clarify.

The man, who had put his right index finger into his right ear, appeared to be trying to push it right through to the other side.

"Master? Yes, I guess so, at least partially, we kind of, ouch, share everything."

There was now blood on the finger

The Vicar, realizing that this was an uphill struggle, persevered valiantly in his attempt to extend the hand of friendship.

"Many of the parishioners know about your move to the area and are I suppose naturally curious, as you see the previous master of Mill House took a Major part in the affairs of the community."

The man turned abruptly and left the drawing room. The Vicar followed him, unsure as to whether he'd been dismissed or not. He followed his host into what had at one time been the scullery adjacent to the kitchens, and then into the servants' sitting room. Men were sticking blocks of white plastic onto the walls.

"Recording studio," the man explained, "we are going to make music here."

The Vicar was very fond of music, but had some doubts as to whether he would enjoy the particular variety produced by these gentlemen. The man had fallen into conversation with one of the workmen and so the Vicar waited for a break, and then wished them the very best of luck in their music making efforts. He took his leave and headed for the front door.

Later sitting in his kitchen with a cup of tea and a biscuit the Vicar's mind moved to the state of the Church. The bells of Somleigh Church, which had called the faithful to prayer since the 16th century, were sorely in need of repair. One of them needed a complete recast, due to a fracture down one side, and the others had problems with dry rot in the mountings. Additionally there was evidence of woodworm in the steeple. All of this meant that the peal of bells was very limited at the moment, and that funds were desperately needed for the repairs. Recently they had even had to contemplate using tape-recorded bells. He had hoped that the new occupants of Mill House might be prepared to help, but after the afternoon's visit he was far from sure of that.

He then remembered that Charlie had recently been made a gardener at the house. And hoping that Charlie might be able to offer additional insight into the new people, he phoned his number and spoke to his wife Maureen. She claimed ignorance of his whereabouts but irritably suggested the pub as being the most likely place look for him.

Putting the phone down, the Vicar debated with himself, which was more in need of a muzzle, Charlie's wife, or Ivan's dog. Not that he would have voiced these thoughts to a living soul, but Maureen had a temper that could curdle milk and a voice that could scare crows at two miles.

He could have said and thought less generous things about Maureen, however being a man of the Cloth he did his very best to see the good in everybody.

Later that evening, he closed his front door and walked through the village past the post office, turning right at the war memorial to the Royal Oak. He chose the door to the lounge and walked in, through the heavy odor of pipe smoke and beer, to the bar, where he was greeted by Joanna.

"Hello Vicar, we don't often see you in here, you here to convert us to temperance or can I get you something to drink?"

It wasn't well known, but Joanna owned the pub as well as a fair proportion of the village. In fact very few people seem to know this. Most people just thought she was just the barmaid. She could have done with a little more clothing on her top half, as with the amount of cleavage she was displaying the Vicar imagined that some of her customers might have difficulties counting their change.

"Good evening Joanna, and no I'm not with the temperance movement tonight, and so I would much appreciate a dry sherry."

Once Joanna had given him his drink, he asked her if she had seen Charlie.

"Yes, round the corner by the fire."

The Vicar paid and made his way around the bar to a corner to where three figures were hunched over a table by the fireplace. A roaring fire coloured the room sepia, and in its light he could see that they were playing dominoes.

"Good evening gentlemen," he started, worried that they would be annoyed at the interruption to their game.

"Evening Vicar," they seemed genuinely pleased to see him.

"Can I have a word?"

"Certainly, pull up a pew." said Charlie pulling a stool from a neighboring table.

"Well, I wondered if I could pick your brains on something Charlie," he began, "it's about the new residents at Mill House. I believe you're working there."

"Yes, started yesterday."

The dominoes were forgotten now, as all three listened closely to what the Vicar might be about to say.

The Vicar told the three men about his visit that afternoon to Mill House and the somewhat odd reception he'd received.

He continued by talking about the bells, and his urgent need for financial support before they came crashing through the Church roof, potentially onto the ringers below.

"So," he went on, "do you think they might be willing to help?"

Charlie scratched his head and thought for a moment before replying.

"I don't suppose it will do any harm to ask, but to be honest; they just don't strike me as the kind of people who would want to help with this. They have a business manager chap, a Richard Fox, who's a bit of a cold fish. He can be quite unpleasant, and they are all London people after all."

"The man I met was I think American," broke in the Vicar.

"Well, that proves it, what do they know about Devon or even the English countryside? I don't suppose they are even Christian Vicar!"

"Are you a regular Church goer?" cut in Archie, and Charlie gave him a filthy look.

"It doesn't sound very hopeful, but to think positively, do you think I should talk to this Richard Fox?" continued the Vicar.

"Why not, I don't hold out much hope, but it wouldn't hurt to try."

"Needs to be thought bout," interrupted Archie, "you'll have to think bout what to say and how to say it! If you get it wrong, you can wait till the cows come home, but you won't get a penny."

It was the Vicar's turn to scratch his head, "That's a point, how do you think we should ask?"

"Well if you just ask him for money, he's gena to say no int he."

"I suppose so, so how do we ask?"

"Got to be something they want to do, something to do with music perhaps or something they are interested in," suggested Charlie.

Ivan had been silent throughout the conversation, so the Vicar asked him what he thought.

"If they offer you anything Vicar, just take it. Two in the bush is worth three in the tree."

"I think I'll get another round," Charlie offered, "what's yours Vicar?"

"Another Sherry would be most kind Charlie,"

Charlie made his way up to the bar, "Three Ferrets and a Sherry please Joanna,"

"Right ho, you'll have to be patient for a minute or two, I'll have to broach another barrel my handsome." She disappeared through the door behind the bar, only reappearing some minutes later.

One by one she filled the three glasses with the foaming liquid, easing back the pump handle as the new barrel came online. She then filled the Vicar's glass from one of the bottles on the wall behind the bar.

Charlie thanked her and then took two trips to transfer the glasses to the table by the fire.

"Many thanks," the Vicar said as Charlie resumed his seat, "so as we were saying…"

He never finished, as the three had raised their glasses to their lips, and then as one man had sipped and recoiled in shock with much spluttering and spitting.

"Bloody hell!" Ivan exploded,

"Hells bells!" Charlie and Archie said together,

Charlie was out of his seat in a second, and closely followed by the other two, and back to Joanna who was reading the Western Morning News.

"Joanna, what's this?" said Charlie, trying not to shout and putting his pint on the bar in front of her.

"Ferrets!" she replied, confused.

"No its not!" Charlie stated, supported by the nodding heads of Ivan and Archie.

"Sure it is, come and have a look if you like."

The Vicar watched as all four of them made their way through the door behind the bar and down the steps. He rose from his seat and walked around the bar to where he could see what was going on below.

Luckily this had never happened with the communion wine, he thought to himself, and imagined having to go back into the vestry to check the label. He'd have to remind himself to take a sip before his parishioners got to it, particularly if Col Smyth was amongst them.

They examined one of the barrels with great care, and then followed the pipe that ran from it, emerging again into the bar where Joanna confirmed that the pipe ended at the pump she had used to pour their drinks.

Joanna had filled a half-pint glass with Ferrets from the pump. She tasted it gently. "I'm not a great Ferrets drinker, but it tastes a bit strange."

"A bit strange!" exploded Ivan, "it's a completely different bloody beer!"

"Well, if you bear with me for a few minutes I'll change the barrel."

She again disappeared through the door behind the bar, and while there she was gone the three men suspiciously sniffed their beers. By this time the commotion had attracted the interest of other drinkers. They were taking it in turns to pour themselves glasses of what ever it was before Joanna had a chance to disconnect the barrel. There was general agreement that it was not Ferrets, but no consensus on what it might be. Some of the less discerning drinkers drank it anyway.

Ivan stood by the bar; still sniffing the contents of his glass, wondering idly if the delivery man had peed in the barrel. But decided it was unlikely, for all sorts of technical reasons.

There was some agreement that the barrel had been mislabeled, and had perhaps come from a different brewery, and been mixed up somewhere along the way. But that couldn't be right as none of the others used oak like Ferrets.

The surreptitious drinkers backed away rapidly from the pump when they heard Joanna's footsteps ascending the staircase to the bar.

"OK, let's have another try," and she fetched a clean glass and started pouring from the new barrel.

She pushed it across to Charlie, who raised it tentatively to his lips, and made a face.

"Smells funny!" he said.

"Come on then, try it," urged Archie.

Charlie raised it again and took a small sip.

A look of distaste appeared on his face as he swirled the fluid around in his mouth, and swallowed it with difficulty.

"No, this isn't right either, tastes worse than Maureen's elderflower wine. Bloody awful!"

Joanna opened the till and proceeded to give Charlie his money back.

"Sorry about that my dear, I've no idea how this could have happened. But don't worry I'll find out from the brewery tomorrow. Can I get you something else to drink?"

"No thanks!" Charlie replied rapidly, fearing something even worse.

The Vicar, whose attempts to get advice from the three had been well and truly shanghaied, realized that his efforts would be better postponed for another evening. He said goodnight to the three, but was not entirely sure that they had heard him, seated around the table again they were discussing the issue in hushed tones.

It was unfortunate that the Church took second place to the local beer, but he'd always tried to work with his parishioners rather than against them. Anyway if he had put that point to them, they might have asked him if cricket and fishing took up rather more time than writing sermons and visiting the sick, and to his eternal shame, they would have been right.

Chapter 4

Mickel Martin, the lead singer for the Cordaxe, was somewhat concerned about the visit from the Priest Guy. He knew that the Church in the UK was not as militant as some US Churches, but he was concerned anyway. The local population in London had caused them very few problems and had pretty much left them alone, unlike the press, which had caused them considerable stress.

It was funny though, because before they had become famous, they had done all the chasing. Chasing record companies, chasing agents, chasing journalists, even chasing fans. Now they were successful, everybody chased them, and Mickel wasn't entirely sure he liked either option.

Some time had flown past since he'd first come to the UK, and he'd spent many years as a session guitarist for other groups. Later, he'd set up Cordaxe with three other guys, who like himself wanted to get away from the migrant lifestyle, and they had started playing their own small gigs. Unfortunately as time went on these gigs have become less frequent, and the venues more grotty and unpleasant.

One night the group had got together at their very lowest ebb to drown their sorrows in vodka and tequila. As they became more and more inebriated they started to develop a tune that they scribbled on to the backs of cigarette packets. Eventually they dragged themselves into taxis and headed back to their respective digs.

A couple of days later Mickel found the remains of the cigarette packets in a coat pocket, and was about to throw them away, when the phone rang and while talking, he absent-mindedly began to look at the scrawl.

Idly toying with the packets he started to put them in order, and once he'd replaced the receiver he read the musical notation on them, and thought it wasn't too bad. So he transposed it on to a clean sheet and a couple of days later, after some rehearsal, played it to the group.

Yes, it had been good, so they had written some lyrics to go with it, and at the next gig it had been very well received. Even the record company to whom they had sent a tape liked it and had agreed to publish.

The inevitable conclusion they had reached was that they wrote best when they were drunk. So shortly after they tried again, and it worked, with the results of the second experiment being even more successful than the first. This second one had got them into the UK Top 40. Quite an achievement considering that some weeks before they had been on the point of giving it all up.

After that they tried various different drinks, ranging from lager and beer, which achieved very poor results, to whiskey and tequila, which worked better. They then moved on to experimenting with mixtures, gin and tequila, whisky and vodka and so on, with gradually improving results, but their big breakthrough and first Top five hit occurred with Marijuana and tequila.

Over the three years since then they had graduated from alcohol to soft drugs including cannabis and then on to morphine, heroin, LSD, and they had now started to experiment with some of the planet's more unusual hypnotics, with ever improving results. So far their best work had been achieved with a mixture of LSD and a snake venom derivative from New Mexico. This had given them a number one hit in both the UK and the US, and had made them all very rich men.

He often wondered where they would all be if it hadn't been for the scribble on the fag packets. Not hounded by the press was one possibility, but then maybe they would have broken up and had to go back to their session lifestyle. But with success came demands for ever more interesting work and that forced them to continue down the creativity pathway, wherever it was to lead.

There were of course problems with this method of composing, not least of which was the effects on their bodies which were wracked with major side effects varying from premature ageing to severe constipation. More recently extremely real and unpleasant visual and auditory hallucinations had become rather problematic.

As a result they had had to start using a padded glass room in which they could conduct experiments in the presence of not only a couple of heavies who could prevent them killing each other if things get a bit hot, but a qualified pharmacist as well. His job was to mix up the drugs and help to deal with some of the more unpleasant side effects, as well as trying to avoid addiction problems.

Another issue of course was getting the stuff into the UK in the first place, but they had found that the more money they were prepared to spend the fewer problems they faced. Additionally as the narcotics became more and more exotic the less interest customs took in them, and they could import samples of the stuff into the UK in many cases completely legally.

OK, they were lucky, as the British police had left them pretty much alone, it was the press which had given them a hard time, hounding them from gig to gig, searching for sensational stories for the front pages. They even gone so far as to set up round the clock surveillance on the London house, and tapped their phones.

There had been a time when he would willingly have kidnapped a press photographer to get their names in the papers. But now it seemed that they could only have the undivided attention of the press when they no longer needed them.

In fact is that been this feeding frenzy which had forced the group to look elsewhere for a base. The last spread they had seen about themselves in the tabloid press had described them as 'the drug band', an image that did little for their record sales, and to which their record company had taken great exception. So far as they knew, the press was aware that they had moved, but as yet, thank God, there was no indication that they had connected them with Mill House.

A large room in the basement of Mill House had been selected for their experiments, as it was not only dry and warm but also large enough to accommodate all of them at the same time. A glass cabin had duly been constructed, all the metal supports padded, and the ceiling and floor cushioned, which left plenty of space in the main body of the room for their minders and the pharmacist. Some days later it was all completed, and the equipment had been installed.

They had used the room for the first time on the evening before the Priest's visit. It gone fairly well, as the chemist had been experimenting for some time with a Bolivian frog, which they were informed produced poisonous juices on its skin. Apparently the local Indians used it to tip their arrows, but if you used too much of the stuff it could have some very unpleasant consequences. The chemist had titrated it down so that there was hardly any of the poison left, and they had taken it in turns to drink a small measure of the stuff. In the morning they had been well pleased once the room had been cleaned and sterilized, and the paper and scrawl retrieved. There was just enough to give them a theme for a new track rather than a completed work, but that was fine as that had been the outcome of many of their experiments.

The chemist had become very excited by the success of the frog extract, and felt that they were heading in a completely new direction. 'A much better side-effect profile' he'd said, and the onset much quicker. They still felt the very rough in the morning, not quite like a normal hangover, but they were used to that, and there was less bruising and no cuts or broken bones this time.

Also, the room had worked well, as a glass bullet proof wall had protected the chemist and the minders, and so what happened on one occasion in London was no longer a risk. The chemist was now waiting for the delivery of a number of toads and frogs from South America. He had spent the last few weeks studying books on poisons and amphibians that he'd borrowed, under his coat, from the library of the London School of Tropical Medicine.

Mickel finished the cigarette he'd been idly toying with, stubbing it out in an ashtray, and rose from the chair in the living room and made his way through the hall to Richard Fox's office. There was no sign of Richard, but leaning over his desk Mickel scrutinized some legal looking documents, something about breweries or something. Mickel took no interest in Richards nefarious outside activities, he'd been a good business manager for them, but all four of them knew that although he was perfectly straight and scrupulous about some things, they had to watch him very closely with others.

When they had taken him on they had had very little money, and consequently would have accepted just about anybody who could do the job. He now knew so much about them that they couldn't get rid of him, and he'd become a fixture, following them about like a dog with a sore paw. They knew he was very mean with money, they had always known this, it was even rumored that he'd had his mother sectioned to a mental asylum so that he didn't have to pay the care home fees.

But he was a very useful negotiator, and could get them a deal far better that they could get themselves, so they kept him on. Every now and then they threw him some crumbs, some spare cash, a small business here and there, but preferred to pretend they knew nothing about it. This meant that if they ever got completely sick of the guy they could get rid of him quickly for fraud, without going through the courts. They knew that he searched their rubbish, looking for anything they threw away which he could sell or use. Some vases had disappeared during the move, and they guessed that he'd sold them someplace, and so they had had them listed on a police stolen antiques list for good measure.

Richard thought that they were so out of their brains on booze and drugs that they couldn't think straight, let alone figure out what he was up to, but they were smarter than he thought, and had him on a loose but strong leash. He returned to the living room and started working on transcribing the musical notation and scribbled words from the previous night's endeavors'.

Chapter 5

Back in the village Maureen had been keeping an eye on things. She liked to do this during the afternoons, because the place was strange and the people were odd, and she only felt safe if she knew what was going on.

When she had been a young woman she had fallen head over heels in love with a local boy, however, her father the Bishop had absolutely refused to let it continue. He was not appropriate, the wrong sort entirely she was told. She screamed and swore and cried until she was sick, but nothing was to any avail. She was sent away to boarding school in Ipswich, and was supervised with great care whilst at home during the holidays.

The boy had been the son of a ribbon weaver in Coventry, who worked in a great factory belonging to Dalton & Barton & Co. His job was to mend the machines when they went wrong, but he was not the son of a gentleman, but the son of a mill worker, and therefore beyond the pale and very much from the wrong side of the tracks. Therefore any liaison between the two was strictly forbidden. In those days classes were not allowed to mix in the way they do these days. It was a miserable time for her, when all her dreams and aspirations were trodden underfoot and destroyed.

The boy eventually married someone else. And she never saw him again. Her father in his wisdom had eventually chosen her a more appropriate husband. She had been maneuvered into what would now be regarded as an arranged marriage with an up and coming young man, the son of an ecclesiastical friend of the Bishop's. He was the son of the Vicar of Stoke near Coventry, a tubby little man with an enormous walrus moustache, who boomed out like a foghorn and hurt her ears when he gave a sermon. The son was affable enough, but there was no liking, and certainly no love between them. He was older than her anyway, she was twenty-four, and he was thirty-three. He had been chosen as the right sort of material, and her father had decided on him as being not only of the right class, but also as being someone who would rise high in the world. She had put her hopes on the success of his career. But too late she discovered that what had at first appeared to be a man with prospects and the drive to achieve great things, in reality proved to be a front. He was lackadaisical, vapid, indecisive, weak, gullible, and in fact had few career prospects if any at all. He worked on the motorways, that were being built throughout the country, but was never to rise high, preferring instead to flounder along at the bottom, and so she spent many years waiting for great things that never came. At first, after the wedding they tried hard for children, but eventually the doctors told them it was not to be. This was a great disappointment for her; she had always wanted to have children, as many as possible. But, some things in our lives never happen the way we would wish. So she found herself trapped in a loveless marriage, with a man she didn't even particularly like, without children, and as the years passed by she became more and more frustrated and unhappy about the direction her life had taken. She often wondered, if she had married the man of her own choosing, would she have had children?

When Charlie retired, he insisted on taking her down to this godforsaken place in the middle of nowhere. She would have been happy to go back to a small house in Coventry, but he insisted, and so she had gone with him. She had gone hoping to make the best of things. But the local people were all idiots, and she wished she had never moved in the first place.

There was not much for her to do in this village full of mad people. She would have preferred to remain in Coventry where she had lived most of her life. At first she had thought she could make a go of it, and find herself a place in the village, but had subsequently discovered that the village was populated by lunatics and the simple minded, who's favorite topics of conversation were beer and sheep. She strongly suspected that incest was the main cause, as they were and always had been too lazy to walk to the next village to find a partner, and choosing instead a convenient close relative.

She watched Ivan through her bedroom window, park his van, stand looking at some sheep over a gate, stare at the pub, walk to the butcher's and examine the joints of meat.

She didn't like Ivan; she had long suspected him of being the center of criminal life in the village. She also knew he'd been watching her, and his glances had

25

always worried her. It had taken him five-and-a-half minutes to do what should have taken 30 seconds, far too long. He was too nosey, and she believed he had been following her. She had got to know quite a lot about Ivan, and had decided that she definitely did not like him. She knew, for example, that his parents had arranged his marriage to a teenage floozy from Bidstable. The girl had been a little strumpet who preferred the bright lights and excitement of the big city, and if she had been allowed would not have married a farmer, but would have remained in Bidstable. The marriage had been disaster from the very beginning. Maureen had extracted every drop of gory detail from those who should have known better than to pass on malicious gossip. She knew how to be nice when she wanted to, pandering to the simple minded. All she had to do was to go and have her hair done in the hairdressers, and the stupid cows who worked there would tell her every piece of juicy vindictive gossip that their feeble brains could divulge.

The girl wouldn't do anything with sheep, was afraid of cows, and wouldn't go near a horse. On their wedding night she had been so appalled by his fumbling attempts at consummating the marriage that she had locked him out of the bedroom and he'd had to sleep in the spare room. Maureen sympathized with the girl; he was a very ugly specimen, big ears, baldhead, and not very nice. The hairdressers had told her that Ivan, also a virgin, had been pretty appalled at the notion of sex, having never been taught the rudiments himself. She was told that Ivan was so terrified by the whole process that he'd never had the courage to try again. And so they had lived in the same house not as man and wife but like brother and sister, able to see but not to touch.

Maureen thought the girl should have walked out at that point. No woman should put up with an unsuccessful marriage, and go through years of unhappiness without having the option of leaving.

With Charlie it was different of course, as there had always been, and still was, a chance she could change him. And she wasn't about to give up now.

Eventually the girl locked herself in the House, only emerging occasionally to feed the chickens, until they were all killed one night after she forgot to lock them in and a fox got the lot of them. Bit their heads off one by one, and left the rest.

Gradually she had become angry, and as her temper got worse and worse, she gave him hell at the end of each day, screaming at him from the top of the stairs. And he'd started to stay away as much as possible. Up very early each day, and home late at night. It reminded her vaguely of Charlie, and she might have though the two cases vaguely similar if it hadn't been for the presence of Ivan and that pub in Charlie's case.

One day he came home to find she blown her brains out in the kitchen with the shotgun, and the dog was eating the bits. The police had been called and had at first thought he'd shot her himself and had locked him up for a few days. Eventually they let him go, which Maureen thought was a big mistake. She was pretty sure that he had shot her, and her evidence was that Charlie had been there the same day, and had walked back through the farmyard after they had taken Ivan away. In one corner lay the remains of the dog; Ivan had blown it to pieces before the police arrived.

After they had let him go he'd returned home, scrubbed the floor and walls until they shone, and had carried on as if nothing happened. Maureen thought it should have been Ivan who was taken out and shot.

She watched him as he came out of the butcher's, a paper wrapped package in his hand. Climbed back in his van, reversed, and drove back down the hill. If she could ever find something, anything, she would let the police know what a big mistake they have made.

There was also the odd thing with Ivan's dog. The women in the hairdressers said he hadn't got the puppy until after his wife's death. But it was the dog's reaction to red colours that made her suspicious. Perhaps it had witnessed something, something to do with blood, and all that barking and snarling was key to it all. She wondered if the police had some way of interviewing dogs, but suspected not.

Recently, she had had at a stroke of luck. While waiting in the doctor's surgery she had happened to pick up a dog-eared copy of a British Airways in-flight magazine. While leafing absent-mindedly through the pages, she had found an advertisement from a London based Security Company. The advert told her that she could listen to people from up to 300 yards away without them being aware of it. When she had got home, she pulled the magazine from her handbag and phoned the number quoted on the advertisement.

Speaking to a man in their offices, she had begun to understand the technology involved. Later that day she had posted a cheque to the London address, and a week later had collected a brown paper package from the post office. She was very much looking forward to her first experiment, and had been playing with the equipment while Charlie was out of the House.

The box had come with five little 'disk' like bugs, which could be placed in discreet places around a building. Each had a tiny battery that would last up to a week, and she could listen to each in turn by turning a dial on the receiver. They were small enough to be hidden under tables, inside lampshades, in fact almost anywhere at all.

As she sat looking out of her window, she was debating with herself where she would place the first bug, the pub seemed an obvious choice, but she had never been in there and so knew little of where Ivan might sit, or she could put it in Ivan's van. Then again, she might be able to sew them into the lining of Charlie's shirt collar.

On reflection the last seems the most sensible strategy, as there was less risk of losing the bug, however was she supposed to follow him wherever he went? No, all she had to do was to wait until he was in the pub with his pal Ivan. Then she would then be able to hear everything that was said, and could do it all from the privacy of her own bedroom.

Leaving the window seat in the sewing room, she went hunting for one of Ivan's shirts, but they were all too old and worn out to be of any use.

Chapter 6

The next morning Joanna rose early. At about half-past nine she phoned the brewery, and after being kept waiting for some minutes managed to speak to Jim Lemon. Jim was the manager of the brewery, and had always been a useful point of contact, usually cheerful and helpful, although she had never met the man.

She asked him about the barrels which caused so much fuss the night before, and he listened patiently what she explained her customers' reactions. Eventually she paused, allowing Jim to give some explanation. She expected to be told that there had been a mix up, but was very surprised by what Jim told her.

"We're under new management Joanna," Jim told her.

"Bought out, lock stock and barrel, new people, not locals. We were ordered to change the beer, because they don't like our brew."

"Do you mean to say that you have changed Ferret Ale without telling anybody?" she asked.

"No-choice, told to change it or they'd bring in new people." explained Jim.

"When did this happen?"

"Couple of weeks ago, but we didn't have enough time to tell anybody, been working flat out to get it done."

Joanna thanked him, and replaced the receiver.

The Brooke family had always owned the brewery, and she never thought that they'd sell it, but it must have gone with the rest of the estate. She contemplated whom she was to tell first. Not being keen to speak with Charlie's wife, as Charlie was almost certainly at work, and Archie was very rarely in, she decided to try Ivan.

She dialed his number and listened to the phone ringing for thirty seconds or so before giving up. Later after a bath and some breakfast she made her way to the village shop to buy milk, bread and a paper. On her way home she saw Ivan's van parked by the lyche gate, and found him doing some repointing behind the vestry.

She told him about her conversation with the brewery manager, and about the change of ownership.

He sat on a gravestone and rubbed his forehead.

Eventually he silently mouthed an expletive and looked up again at Joanna.

"We'll just have to find out who's bought it, and see if we can't persuade them to change it back again," he mused, "I think we had better pay a visit to this Jim Lemon. Can you get away today?"

"Yes, I have to open up at 12, but I could get away after 2."

"Right, I'll pick you up then. Can you let him know we're coming?"

Joanna agreed, and retraced her steps through the graveyard. As she closed the lyche gate behind her, she could see Ivan still sitting on the stone staring vacantly into space.

Ivan wasn't thinking about beer. He had just seen the Brigadier-General's car go past, heading for the river, and was wondering where Archie was, and whether or not he'd time to warn him before he was meant to meet Joanna.

Joanna found him waiting as promised outside the pub shortly after 2pm.

"Sorry to keep you, some people don't know the meaning of last orders."

"No problem,"

They made their way through the narrow lanes towards South Moxton. Sometimes the van seemed to be in a tunnel, as the hedges that grew some 12 feet above them, and met in the middle. They descended into the Taw valley and followed the river for a while, where below them in the silver water Tarka the Otter had once played. They then turned off the Bidstable Road at Umberlake and made their way across the river over a thousand year-old bridge and up the hill towards South Moxton.

The brewery itself was hidden amongst the buildings that fringed the high street, hidden only by the hotel and a market hall. They parked the van in the cattle market car park, and crossed the road to the brewery entrance. The metal grill door was locked and bolted, lorries having been and gone many hours earlier, and so they made their way up the steps to the administrative office door with its peeling green paint.

They pressed the buzzer, and waited for some minutes until a man in khaki overalls opened up. He took them upstairs to Jim Lemon's office, which they were surprised to find was like a Victorian study, with bookshelves lined with ancient legers. A great slab of a desk filled the center of the room, and behind it a little man sat watching them as they entered.

He stood up and introduced himself, and they shook hands.

A tiny window, so stained by age that she could hardly see through it at all, interrupted the shelving on one side of the room. Above them a single bulb illuminated the room poorly, so that only the desk could be described as being well lit, and everything else in the room lay in heavy shadow.

The brewery was an old one, and Jim had worked there since he was a boy. Before him his father, grandfather and great grandfather had worked for Ferrets. He had joined just before they had replaced the old dray horses with a lorry. He had missed them, but accepted that the lorry could do more miles for less money. He saw no reason to change for change's sake. The pipes were all the original copper; the vats were still oak, as were the barrels. Most of the other breweries had long switched to aluminum.

Likewise the brewery was largely unaltered, and Jim was sure even his great grandfather would recognize much of it. Most of all, there was no way on God's earth he was going to modernize his office.

"I suppose you'll hear about the beer," he said, stating the obvious, "I'm very much afraid you've had a wasted journey, it's all been laid down, decided, signed for, and fixed."

"But what do you think Jim?" asks Joanna,

"Well, I can't say I like it, but I don't think we've got a choice in the matter, at least if we want to keep our jobs. Don't misunderstand me though, I could have retired years ago, but if I had, Ferrets would have closed, and it's just the same now."

Ivan, looking more closely at Jim Lemon had great difficulty in guessing his age. He was a short little dumpy man, with a wide mouth, and the habit of swallowing between sentences. He reminded Ivan vaguely of a toad.

"They have wives and children to support, and without this, they'll be on the social," Jim continued.

"But this new beer is absolutely disgusting," interrupted Ivan.

"Oh I know, I agree with you, it is rather vile isn't it!"

"So why do you make it?"

"Well, we have no choice, as I told Joanna here on the telephone, we didn't get a say, he just came and told us what to put into the brew, tasted it later and told us to get on with it. He says this is what they like in London, and that we shouldn't be bothered by the tiny local market, as that would die eventually anyway."

Joanna who had been thinking silently for some minutes asked, "Who is this chap anyway, is he a brewing man?"

"Oh no, doesn't seem to know much about brewing, he's a businessman as far as I can make out. I've got his business card here somewhere," and he proceeded to rummage through the upper draws of the desk.

"Got it," he said, pulling a white card from one of the drawers, and handed it to Joanna.

Joanna examined the card, turning it over and held it under the light to see it better. Ivan leant forward to try and read the inscription, and knew the name as soon as he saw it. 'Richard Fox', it said in gold lettering.

"Ah," exclaimed Ivan, "Charlie's been talking about him, he one of those new people at Mill House."

"So far as I know, he's the manager of a company based in London," interjected Jim.

"Yes, he's also the business manager for a pop group, obviously got his fingers in lots of pies," mused Ivan, "Jim, can you tell us the name of the company he works for?"

"No problem," and Jim proceeded to search through his desk drawers again, eventually reappearing with a compliment slip.

"This is them," he said and handed it to Ivan.

Ivan took the offered slip of paper and read the company's name, then handed it to Joanna. 'Foxtradic limited' it said.

They thanked Jim and made their way back to the van.

On the way home they speculated on Richard Fox and his acquisition of Ferrets.

"There is something funny going on," Joanna speculated, "it just doesn't seem right, what with him seeming to be a business manager, but at the same time buying the brewery. Something about it stinks!"

"I'm not sure I understand it all, but I agree it's a bit odd for him to be taking over the brewery when he supposed to be a pop promoter or something, but I suppose he's just got private interests."

"So if he's got private interests, and can afford to buy a brewery, what's he doing working as a manager for a pop group?"

"Buggered if I know!" Ivan said.

"Well I think we'd better find out."

Chapter 7

Later that afternoon, with plenty of time left before she had to worry about opening the pub up, Joanna made a couple of phone calls to her brokers, Nigel Trout in London and Tim Weaver in Exeter.

She supposed it was a natural talent she had for building a network, and for knowing more about what was going on around her than people supposed. As a single woman it gave her confidence, like a kind of psychological radar. Sometimes she preferred to play the dumb blonde, and it worked in her favor most of the time. She often claimed ignorance when someone was pontificating on about something she knew about. That was how she picked up some of her best information.

She had drive as well; in fact she had always had the desire to win. Some of her earliest memories had been about fighting for her corner of the school playground. When her mother had died she had been ten, and could have given up like her father. But she decided, in a childlike way, to take over from her mother, and as her father slipped gradually into depression and alcoholism, she became stronger and stronger. They had the lease of Down Farm, and ran it as best they could, but times were hard. There was no electricity, and the only water came out of the pump in the yard. They had a stove in the kitchen that heated the house, and it had been one of her chores to keep it burning at all times.

The house was thatched, and even though it had seen better days and had grass growing thickly on the North end, it was warm in the winter and cool in the summer. But when the wind was in the east, it blew down the chimney and the smoke from the stove sometimes filled the whole house, making it almost impossible to breathe.

Her days were long, she had to rise at 5am, and in the winter the yard in front of the house was like an ice rink, and getting the cattle across to the milking shed first thing in the morning was an un-missable experience.

Her father did recover in the end, but it took five years and he only pulled himself together after the episode with the bull. She had been mucking out, and had thought him well secured behind a barrier, but he'd got through it, gently pushed her to the ground, and put his horn through her stomach.

She was in hospital for six months, but when she got home he was off the booze and back to his old cheerful self.

She glanced up at a carved stone on her windowsill, almost hidden by bottles of hair spray. It was all she had left of Down Farm. It was a chip of an ancient gravestone, which she had found in the yard one year, and kept as a good luck charm. She had sold the farm after her father died, and had started buying property round the village, including the pub, and a few other places.

Later Nigel rang from London, Foxtradic was a newly created company, and Richard Fox and an accountant were registered as directors. At first he'd thought that it might just be a shell company, perhaps owned by the record production company, but 100% of the paid-up share capital was registered and owned by Richard Fox.

He had also discovered that Fox was an employee of the Cordaxe group. He said he could find nothing on the purchase of Mill House, but quite a lot on the group's finances and share dealings.

Later that evening the extension from the flat rang in the bar; and her contact in Exeter told her that he'd talked to Companies House, and had been told that Ferrets was not the only business that had been bought by Foxtrad in the last few months, and both had been purchased for nominal prices, from Cordaxe.

Shortly after the pub opened that evening, Ivan overtook Charlie on his way to the pub. Ivan reversed his muddy van into an empty space, and then accompanied Charlie into the bar.

Archie was already there, and unusually for him was seated at the bar, deep in conversation with Joanna. They stood for a few moments while Ivan explained the events that had taken place earlier that day.

Later they took their accustomed seats by the fire. For a while the three men sat in silence, staring depressingly at the ciders in front of them. They watched Archie trying to light his pipe with damp tobacco, and contemplated their course of action as he sucked at the stem whilst applying his lighter optimistically to the bowl.

Archie was contemplating having fought a world war so that musicians could play appalling music and he could drink ghastly flat cider.

Charlie was wondering what the notoriously superstitious Mrs. Tirrall was going to say when she found a crow sitting on eggs in her hen house. It had seemed such a waste just leaving it dead by the roadside.

Ivan was wondering if the Brigadier-General had spotted Archie, his rod and the fish as he slipped away through the trees.

Eventually it was Charlie who broke the silence.

"So, what are we to do then?"

"Buggered if I know," returned Ivan, "it doesn't look as if there's much we can do."

For while Charlie played with his cap; twisting and turning it absent-mindedly between his hands.

"What if I went out to other pubs searching for old formula Ferrets, and buy the barrels when I find them?" he asked.

"Just think what the landlords would do to you if they worked out what you were up to," said Ivan.

Charlie was worrying more about what Maureen would do if he turned up with twenty barrels.

"Anyway, all the other pubs will be in the same situation as us by now," Ivan added.

Charlie took a tentative sip of the cider, replaced the glass on the table and stared at it suspiciously, "could we buy him out?"

"Unlikely, but even if we did, he'd probably take us to the cleaners," Ivan responded.

After a few minutes Joanna finished serving a tractor driver from Bealand, and came over to join them, adding a log to the fire as she sat down.

She told them about her conversation with her brokers, and the ownership of Ferrets.

"Well, any ideas?" she asked, studying them by turns.

"We're stumped, there just doesn't seem to be any way out," Charlie replied, "if Richard Fox owns Ferrets, beyond just asking him, we can't see any way to get him to change the brew back."

Archie, who had finally managed to get his pipe to light, snorted through a thick cloud of smoke, "Need to get rid of the bloody man, he's never going to do anything sensible!"

Joanna, the still clear voice of reason, shook her head and rejected his implied proposal outright. "No, nothing like that Archie please, however there must be some way of persuading him to sell it."

But before they could ask what she meant, she had to return to the bar to serve a couple of guns just returned from the Holocombe shoot.

Later that week the Vicar decided to make the long postponed phone call to Richard Fox. He had to try a number of times as the phone was either continually engaged or there was no answer at all. When he did finally get through to the man, Fox had just returned from the drawing room where he'd been taking some abuse from the group.

They had discovered his purchase from the estate of a hair dressing business in

Chulmleigh for a thousand pounds. They were threatening to have a valuation done, and Fox knew very well that if it was done it would come out with an approximate price somewhere in the region of thirty thousand which would not please the group. Unbeknown to him they were just having some fun, and actually had no intentions of doing anything of the sort. But they enjoyed pulling his tether and were thoroughly enjoying themselves.

When Fox heard the phone ringing in his study, overcame with relief, he used it as an excuse to make his escape.

He picked up the receiver, "Yes," he snapped.

The Vicar on the other end, having been trying so persistently to speak to someone was rather startled by the violent response and instead of launching into the well-rehearsed and fluent proposition, began by stuttering, quite badly, which didn't help the matter in the least.

"Um, err, um," he started "it's the err, um, the Vicar here from the err village um."

"Yes," snapped Fox, "what do you want?"

The Vicar, who was used to some degree of civility, was further rattled by the man's rudeness.

"It's err, I was phoning to see if um, err we could get your help with um, err, with the Church."

"What about the Church?" snapped Fox.

"Well it's you see," the Vicar continued, "we need some work doing on the err, bells in the tower because of the state of the err…"

He never got any further.

Fox snapped back at him, "We came down here to get away from people, not to get mixed up in your local community; we are not interested in your local events, tombolas, raffles, fundraising, bells or anything else. We want nothing to do with any of it."

"Well," continued the Vicar, clutching at straws, "I was just thinking perhaps…."

The phone was slammed down at the other end.

The Vicar winced, removed it from his ear and stared at the offending article in some shock. Charlie had said he was a difficult character to deal with, but now he knew the worst of it. He gingerly replaced the phone in the cradle, and rubbed his tired eyes.

'Beyond the pale,' he thought to himself, and then wondered why he was so shocked by a bit of rudeness, when Jesus had been whipped and crucified.

His wife bustled in, with a fresh vase of daffodils from the garden; she placed them on a table, and straightened the blooms.

"Anything the matter dear?" she asked.

"It's just that I was hoping to get some assistance with the bells from the new people at Mill House," he said, "but the chap I spoke to was extremely rude, so it doesn't look like we'll get any help from that quarter."

34

"Well," she replied, "I'm sure you'll think of something," and bustled out again. He wished he had as much confidence in his own abilities as she had in him. Later she brought him a cup of tea, which he drank as he assessed his options. He didn't see he had much chance with this Fox character, the man was obviously an intractable rogue. And although it might be possible to reform the character like that, it might be a long job. He wondered if he could approach any of the other people at Mill House. He knew they were musicians but beyond his short meeting with Mickel Martin, he knew nothing about them at all. Mind you, he thought to himself, the man he'd met was a strange enough character in his own right, with all that business with his ear, very odd indeed. Eventually he thought that perhaps some advice might come in handy and he attempted to phone Ivan at Greenly Barton, but there was no response. Ivan, he guessed was probably out on his farm. He thought about phoning Joanna, but felt he'd better speak to Ivan first. Although she had some good ideas, it wasn't always very easy to talk to her, as she had her own views on things like this. Anyway Ivan had been extremely helpful once or twice in fundraising, and so he had a suspicion that Ivan would be able to solve his problem or, at least, had a better chance of it.

He put a coat on, told his wife he was just going out for a short drive, "going to go and see if Ivan's about," he explained.

When he got to Greenly Barton, there was no sign of life at all and he assumed he'd had a wasted journey. He turned the car round and headed back up the drive to the lane. Just as he was approaching the junction, Ivan's van appeared round the corner. They drew to a halt facing each other. The Vicar climbed out and went round to the passenger side of Ivan's van and leant in the open window.

"Hello Vicar," said Ivan, "what can I do you for?"

"Well I just wanted to keep you informed as to the state of play with the Church fund and the people at Mill House."

"Oh yes, tell all," Ivan responded.

"I phoned tat chap, what's his name, Richard Fox, this afternoon, and he was extremely unpleasant I'm afraid."

"That doesn't surprise me," consoled Ivan, "what did he actually say?"

"He said they didn't want to be involved in any local events, and then he put the phone down on me!"

"Well that's a dead duck then," said Ivan,

"I suppose so," admitted the Vicar, "unless you can think of a better tactic?"

"Mmm," mused Ivan.

"I did think about contacting some of the other members of the band," admitted the Vicar, "but having met one of them, I don't think the others will be any more amenable to our suggestions."

"No you are probably right," admitted Ivan, "we'll have to think of something better than that. I'll do some thinking and get back to you in a couple of days.

Now hang on a minute I'll reverse up," and he reversed back into the lane. As they passed each other they waved and the Vicar headed back to the Vicarage. Ivan returned to the farm, got Pitch out of the back of the van and put her into the Nissan hut. He fed and watered her, and then went in to change. He'd been down by the river that day, looking at the cattle in the lower field and his trousers had got very muddy. He changed, returned to the van, and drove back up to the Oak. When Ivan entered the pub, he discovered that Charlie was already there and Archie drifted in shortly afterwards. They greeted each other, and had a somewhat protracted conversation as to what they were going to drink.

Archie said he was too old to change, and that he was going to try the ferrets again, just in case. The other two asked for half pints of cider.

"Dry please," Charlie ordered.

When he returned to the table he placed the three glasses round the table, and sat down on the stool. Ivan told the other two what the Vicar had told him earlier that day.

So they agreed, "Not much chance of getting any joy out of that lot then."

"No," agreed Ivan, "they are an intractable bunch. We might even see them putting up barbed wire around the house."

Charlie agreed, "Yes," he said, "they don't seem to want to have anything to do with anybody in the area. The only way the Vicar might get any money out of them is bribery or blackmail."

Ivan and Archie stared depressedly at their glasses.

Suddenly Archie grinned, lifted his head, and said, "We could allez frighten the buggers out!"

"Eh," asked Charlie, "what do you mean?"

"Well, just a thought," admitted Archie.

"Go on, tell us what you've got in mind," prompted Ivan.

"No, not yet," Archie deferred, "I've got a little bit of homework to do first." And that was the end of that particular conversation. And the other two were left to guess at Archie's idea. Whatever it was Archie had up his sleeve, he wasn't going to tell them yet anyway.

Ivan went over and had a chat with Joanna later, told her what the Vicar had said, and she said pretty much the same as the other two.

"I'm afraid the Vicar's not going to get much joy out of them," she agreed, "however," she added, "I don't think it would do any harm to go and have another word with Jim over in South Moxton."

"I agree," he admitted, "if nothing else, at least we could find out a little bit more about what's going on."

Chapter 8

Archie rose very early the following morning, and was up and about with the lights on in his tiny kitchen by 4 o'clock; well before the cock even contemplated crowing. He usually rose early, normally 6 o'clock, and listened to the farming program on radio 4. But today, there was a special reason to be up and about early. He had a quick bowl of corn flakes, and made his way out to the Morris. He opened the rear doors, and took some equipment from his lean-to and threw it into the back. Next he took some balls of twine and a torch from one of the shelves, and pushed it into the pockets of his Barbour.

The old man had told him to be prepared, which as a child he'd regarded as a scouting instruction. Later he'd learnt that in the first war it meant having a supply of toilet paper when you most needed it. Over the years the old man's saying had come to mean many different things to Archie. The most important was having a good excuse for the magistrate as to why he was on someone else land with a gun and a bag of pheasants.

He started the car, and followed the lane for about three miles until he reached the three bridges. He parked the Morris, and walked up the spine of the ridge that overlooked Mill House. It was quite a battle getting to the top, as the hill was thickly clothed in Holly that interspersed the trunks of the ancient oaks. Eventually he reached a point at which he could overlook Mill House, and he peered down on the gray slate roof fifty feet below. The faintest wisps of smoke were emerging from a chimney, and he could see a few cars parked on the driveway. But there was no sign of life, no lights, and no noise.

"Good," he thought to himself. He then took a bearing with his stick from the back of what he took to be the kitchens, facing into the rock below him, and then swung the stick across to the far side of the ridge.

Here a tributary of the Torrage followed the valley to meet the main river by the three bridges. He lined the stick up on a birch tree on the far side of the ridge, and walked towards it.

When he got close he had to watch his step, because the slope of the hill was extremely steep. There were ancient quarries cut in to the hill face, which made it extremely treacherous for the unwary. When he got to the point at which his ancient legs found the slope too steep he took the ball of bright orange binder twine from his pocket, attached it to a convenient stick and threw it out as far as he could over the gap. It disappeared rapidly over the edge of the hill below him.

He'd been taught basic surveying by the army, so long ago now that it seemed like a dream. For a few months he'd become rather good at laying mine fields in the desert. But when they tried to find them again he discovered that he was better at laying the mines than at finding them again.

He retraced his steps down the hill and back through the Holly. When he got back to the Morris, he opened the back, and took out an implement, somewhat like a pickaxe, which had long ago been used by African farmers for digging their fields.

He supposed the old man had brought it back from the Boer war. Presumably the Boars hadn't needed it any more after the British had educated them out of their misguided impression that farming was a good way to feed people.

The old man had said that at first the Boers had educated the British that the best way to surprise a Boer with a rifle, was to break rank and head in the opposite direction as quickly as possible.

Later they had put the Boer women and children into camps, where they had educated them about dysentery and typhoid and cholera.

It had a flat blade on one side and a short spike on the other. Ideal for what he had in mind.

He made his way up the sodden track that followed the base of the hill, parallel with the river. It was wet enough at this time of year, but during the spring it was occasionally flooded to a depth of several feet. As he walked he peered at the side of the hill and soon the ancient quarries appeared through the dim morning light on his left. Although the twine had seemed bright and easy enough to see when he'd extracted it from his pocket, he couldn't find it. The sun was coming up, and the dawn chorus had started, but the light was still weak. Eventually completely unable to find the twine, he had to guess, and walked into the largest of the quarries. This was where the majority of the stone for the village had come from, probably three or four hundred years before. Possibly even the stone for Mill House itself. The floor of the quarry was carpeted in a deep spongy mass of light green sphagnum moss, and his boots sunk up to the gunnels as he plugged his way towards the far corner. A fox ran from cover and disappeared across the track toward the river.

Peering up at the dimly lit quarry walls he spotted the orange binder twine, hanging in the branches of an ancient elder that clung tenaciously to the quarry wall.

From there on in he knew exactly what to do. He went back through the moss and the mud to the path, and approaching the quarry wall, proceeded to tap the quarry wall with his pick. This was necessary, because much of it was thickly coated in moss and slime, some of it seeming to bubble straight out of the rock itself.

Tap, tap, tap went the sharp end of the pick, but there was no evidence of any gaps or fissures. Eventually he got to the very furthest corner where the quarry turned a right angle. The wall then turned back towards the main path. Here there was a stout young oak hanging on to the wall itself. It looked as if it had been coppiced at some point in the past, and he had to force his way through its branches to get to the rock face beyond. It was more thickly carpeted with moss than most of the other areas, and as he tapped, the pick sank softly into the mossy layer. A glimmer of a smile came over Archie's face.

"I wonder," he said to himself, and turned the pick round. With the flat blade he proceeded to scrape the moss away from the wall. It came away in great lumps, and as it fell at his feet he had to move his boots to stop it falling into

38

them. Fairly quickly he was able to uncover a fissure in the rock; it must have been about a foot and a half to two feet wide, and narrowed to a point above his head. The moss here was extremely thick, and it took him some time to break through, but eventually he found himself looking into a void beyond. After about fifteen minutes he was then able to squeeze through the narrow gap into the darkness of the cavern.

Fishing the torch from his pocket, he switched it on and found himself looking down a narrow cave that disappeared into the hill in front of him. He walked in, gingerly holding the torch in forward in one hand and the pick in the other hand. It was very difficult to see, once some twenty feet in he very nearly tripped over the remains of an ancient wooden wheelbarrow. But once past this, the floor seemed to level out and the walking became much easier.

In fact the fissure widened until it was almost twenty feet across. After another few feet it narrowed down again, and his way was barred by thick accumulations of spider web, which he pulled aside using the pick, and forced his way through. Finally, he found his way barred by a wall, thickly coated in ash and spider silk. He gently scraped at it with the flat blade of the pickaxe to reveal a wooden plank. He proceeded to uncover the planking, taking care not to make too much noise. And yes, what he found underneath the debris of ash, soot, spider web and the dirt of ages was the back of a cupboard.

'So the old man was right after all,' he said to himself.

He had always wondered about the old man's story. His mother had said she though the larder must have contained a big heavy jug of cider, which the old man had had to empty before the larder could be moved. He remembered lots of smoke and the old man's pipe catching fire after his mother had made that particular comment.

It took him another twenty minutes to free up the back of the cupboard, and once he could see the majority of it he found that the old man hadn't secured it in place.

"Well that's a stroke of luck," and gently he put pressure on it - to see if it would move. At first it didn't. So he sat on the ground, placed both feet against the base of the cupboard, gently pushed, and after a second or two it began to shift. He shuffled forward slightly, got himself a few inches closer to the cupboard and repeated the procedure. Within a few minutes he'd pushed the cupboard about a foot away from the wall, which meant that he was able to peer around the edge and see into the scullery beyond.

It was dark within, but there was just enough light filtering in from somewhere to allow him to see walls lined with bottles and containers. It was the old scullery; old man Brook had used it for years. Jams, pickles, and the like lined its walls in jars. They had not thought to sell them at the sale, and they were still there. He wondered if they were still edible and couldn't see why not, but he quickly put the thought from his mind, breaking and entering, wasn't something he did every day of the week.

39

He removed his boots, so as not to leave tell-tale-traces, and stepped gingerly around the cupboard. It wasn't terribly big, the old man had said it was bigger, but perhaps his memory had been playing tricks on him. About three and a half feet wide he guessed, and about six foot high, neatly concealing the crevice. Light was filtering through the fissure from the dawn beyond. Just enough to be able to see into the fissure, and get an impression of the scullery. He made his way softly across the room to the door and placed his ear against it. The time was nearly six o'clock, and the house was completely silent. He gently lifted the latch and peered cautiously into the corridor. No lights, no noise. Absolute silence. He closed the door gingerly behind him and made his way back to the cupboard. Now, how to replace the cupboard in its original position? From within, just a short push would have done the job, but from the far side it was slightly tricky. He took another length of binder twine from the pocket of his Barbour, and looped it round the base of the cupboard. He then went back into the fissure beyond, seated himself on the rough stone floor, and with both hands gently heaved on the string. He found that by altering hand positions and placing the left hand string in one hand and the right in the other, he could gradually tug the cupboard back into its original position. He then let go of the right hand loop of the string, and pulled it back through with the right.

There were some things in the cupboard, but fortunately it was not too heavy to move. Additionally, he'd taken great care not to leave any evidence of his passing, and so hoped that any repeated entry would be as silent as the first. He replaced the string in his pocket, and taking the torch from his teeth, retraced his steps using the pick to feel his way.

Chapter 9

"CHARLIE!" screamed Maureen.

Charlie leapt like a startled goat. He had been trying to get to the front door unobserved, but the faint creak of a floorboard was well known to her by now, and he'd not learnt to avoid it.

"Where are you going?" she bellowed, "Oh, um, just out." he replied.

"Where to?" she persisted.

"Oh, I thought I'd pop into the pub and have a word with Ivan," he admitted.

"You shouldn't spend so much time with that man," she accused, "he's up to no good."

"He's alright," said Charlie, "he's a nice enough chap; I don't see what you've got against him."

"For once in your life, why don't you open your eyes and see what's going on around you," Maureen complained. "You're too good natured, people take advantage of you, they'll get you into trouble, I know they will."

"You're over reacting again Maureen," Charlie said, "look I'll be back later."

And he slipped rapidly out of the door, closing it softly behind him.

As he made his way up the road, Charlie wondered how he'd come to get himself lumbered with a wife like Maureen. Perhaps he'd done something very bad in a past life, and Maureen was his punishment. Whatever it was, he guessed it must have been pretty awful.

Maureen went up the stairs, and sat down behind the net curtains in the sewing room. From there she could see him walking up the High Street towards the Royal Oak.

"Right," she said to herself, "with him out of the way I can get down to business."

She went back to her bedroom, and extracted the brown paper package from beneath her underclothes in the bottom drawer. She took it into the sewing room and un-wrapped it. She'd opened it before, and knew exactly what to do. So taking the tiny bugs out of their foil wrapping she placed them in front of her on a shelf.

Recently she had been very generous, and had bought him some very nice new shirts in Torrington. Taking the first one, she gently undid the packaging, and taking a sharp knife proceeded to cut the thread that held the lapels together. Once she had made enough of a space she slipped one of the bugs into the left hand side.

"Remember - the left side," she said to herself, "I don't want to wash the things." Delicately she sewed the lapel up again, so that he wouldn't be able to spot any evidence of her action. She repeated this action with the right hand side and slipped in a similarly sized button. When she had sewn that one up, she repeated the procedure with the remaining five shirts.

"That will do it," she thought.

Then she turned the radio on in the sewing room, and carrying the contents of the box she went into the bedroom. Then she seated herself on her bed, placed the batteries into the back of the receiver unit, and switched it on. At first she could hear nothing, but as she rotated the dial she could hear the radio coming through loud and clear. She stood up, crossed to the door and closed it. She then went back to the tuner and again listened again. Yes she could definitely hear the music coming through very distinctly. The instructions said each of the bugs had a slightly different frequency so taking a piece of paper she wrote down the frequency of each in turn. So she would know exactly which one to listen to on which day. Charlie didn't take any notice of when his clothes were washed, so she could probably keep him in the same shirt for a whole week, but would have to be careful that she didn't go and damage them by washing them. That would mean un-sewing one shirt a week, which was easily managed.

The next day, Charlie found a new shirt laid out for him. He never even noticed the buttons in the lapels and put the thing on completely unawares.

She wondered if there was any way she could have bugged Ivan, but the chances were that would be extremely difficult. The man knew she didn't like him in the

Charles Joynson

least, so anything from her to him would be viewed with great suspicion.
No, Charlie would have to do, and yes she would have to listen to lots of inane
drivel, but there was just a chance she might pick up on what was really going
on. She wondered what it was about Ivan that annoyed her so much, but she
was certain he was up to something. And he would get Charlie into trouble if
she wasn't careful. He was a nasty piece of work she was sure of it, that business
with his wife, the police had really fallen down there. If she taped him, the
police would be able to use it as evidence. Unfortunately the equipment she
bought didn't have a tape recorder with it, which meant that she would have to
get the police to catch him red handed. That was perhaps not as easy as she had
originally hoped.
That evening as Charlie made his way into the Royal Oak, she sat in the sewing
room, with the curtain drawn, so that the light from within couldn't be seen,
and placed the headphones to her ears. She heard him closing the bar door, and
saying, "evening," to somebody who crossed his path, and the scraping of chairs
and then muffled greetings and ordering at the bar. She was somewhat surprised
he didn't order Ferrets.
"Cider, he has taken to cider," she said to herself, "I wonder why?" Then there
seemed to be a long rambling conversation about clothes and hats. She couldn't
make head or tail of it. Was she overhearing somebody else's conversation? But
although mystified, she continued to listen, wondering what was going on, and
beginning to distrust the equipment.
Then she recognized her husband's voice, "Yes, but I don't want to wear the
damned thing," he said clearly. "But that's the best way," another voice said.
"I've already got it," somebody else said, that sounded like Ivan.
"And I'm not wearing bloody tights!" she heard her husband say quite loudly.
All this was very strange indeed, there was something really very odd going on.
Had her husband taken to wearing women's clothes? She'd heard about people
like that! Although she continued to listen, she couldn't make any more sense
out of what was going on. Eventually it was agreed that they were going to meet
the following day at Ivan's house. But for some reason Charlie sounded
extremely unhappy about it. She heard him say something about something not
fitting properly.
"What didn't fit properly?" she wondered.
"But you're the only one tall enough," somebody said, and then the battery
seemed to die and she had difficulty hearing what was going on.
In fact, the gas fire had been lit in one corner of the pub and it had disrupted
the signal. Charlie, disgruntled, persuaded Archie to buy the next round.
"I don't very much like cider anyway, but it's better than nothing," he said.
Even Archie had eventually given up the Ferrets, most of which had remained
untouched.
"Bloody filthy stuff," he admitted, "I'm not touching that again, not till they
change it back. I think someone's dog's been a bit too close to the barrels."

42

Maureen brooded over the snatches of conversation, until Charlie reappeared that evening. She didn't ask him anything, being wise enough not to give herself away.

"Are you out tomorrow?" she asked.

"I might be," he said, "thinking of going down to Ivan's place just for a while."

"What for?" she asked, trying to wheedle the answer out of him.

"Oh nothing, just to help with some posts and stuff." he said.

"I thought you were supposed to be working at Mill House,"

"I get Wednesday afternoons off," he admitted.

"Oh," she said, "I didn't know that."

That was another thing she would have to remember. Wednesday afternoons were a good time to tune in.

The following afternoon, the three men met at Ivan's house. Charlie and Archie arrived at about the same time, and Ivan went out and greeted them.

"Come on in," he said.

But he led them, instead of into the house, into one of the outlying sheds. They followed him into a dusty storage room and he flicked a switch on. It had once been used to house cattle, probably a small dairy herd, but long ago had been given a wooden floor, and now the whole room was littered with storage boxes, old musical instruments, various forms of farming tools, bags, sacks bulging in strange places, and all manner of other things. Some of it reached as high as the roof.

"It's this box over here," Ivan said, and the other two helped him to heave it out. It was an old wooden trunk, the type you used to see schoolboys taking to school with them. There were old battered labels on the lid addressed to a school in Somerset.

"Let's get it out a bit further so we can see what's in it," Ivan said.

And they pulled it out to the center of the room. Ivan then raised the lid and inside they could see the puritan hats he'd talked about. Archie pulled the first one out and stuck it squarely on Charlie's head. "Fits you to a tee!" he said. Charlie grunted. Next the costume was pulled out and even Charlie had to admit it was too long and narrow for either of the other two men to get into.

"Git your trousers off then," Archie said with a huge grin on his face.

"Oh God," said Charlie, "do I have to?"

"Yes come on, get on with it," Ivan said, "haven't got all day."

Charlie stripped down to his underpants and socks, and was then given the costume to put on, "stockings, bloody stockings," he muttered to himself. The other two helped him to dress in the costume and then placed the hat on his head. They then stood back to admire their handiwork. Gradually their faces cracked up and they began to roar with laughter.

"Tis no good," admitted Archie, "I can't stand it; I'll never get through that cave with a straight face with you in that costume!"

"I don't like it," admitted Charlie, "I don't want to wear this bloody thing; I look like a right fool." "Better than that," admitted Archie, "it's the funniest thing I've seen for years. We'll have to have you in the pantomime this Christmas!"

"Its wonderful," agreed Ivan, "but probably too good for any haunting, if we stick him in the old house in that, we are more likely to get them all to die of laughter than anything else."

Charlie rapidly pulled off the costume, threw it back into the truck, and put his clothes back on again.

"Haven't you got anything better?" he asked. Ivan wrinkled his brow and thought about it.

He was trying to recollect where the costumes came from, remembering finally his interest in a young lady from the Torrington players, who had batted her long eye lashes at him, and enticed him into playing a spear carrier in the local theatre.

She was the society's recruiting officer of course, and he was just the latest in a long line of young men she had enticed to play minor roles.

The worst of it was that he caught her having relations with the director in the costume rooms.

He had fled and had been too embarrassed to return the costumes.

"I might have," he admitted, "but err, I can't get to it."

"We'll help," agreed Charlie, hoping for any alternative which would get him out of having to wear that bloody awful costume.

"All right, let's put this box back first," And the three of them heaved it back into position in the corner of the room. They then turned off the light and re-traced their steps across the farmyard. Ivan led them into another building, an old barn. On one side there was a huge pile of hay bales, but on the other there was a small lock up room. He extracted a key out from under a brick, and opened the door. The rusty old lock let them through eventually and they entered an ancient storage room. Once inside, they found it was even more stuffed with boxes and bags than the stable.

"I think it's in here somewhere," Ivan said, "I haven't seen it for years, but I thought this was where it was." And so they began to take the lids off boxes and undo bags, peering into old containers, pulling out packing materials, looking as Ivan had said for costumes of any sort. It was hot and dusty work, and took them almost an hour to find what they were looking for.

"What the bliddy hell's this?" Archie asked at one point. "Oh that's err, a banner from the church," admitted Ivan.

"What the hell are you doing with it?" asked Archie.

"I don't know; something the old man had I suppose." It was a regimental flag and must have hung in the church originally. How it had got down to Greenly Barton he couldn't think. Another box contained a lamp; another a vase; another was full of wine glasses; another contained an empty case for a shotgun.

"Why don't you sell some of this stuff," asked Charlie, "and make a bit of money?"

"Oh I couldn't be bothered," said Ivan, "It's too much like hard work. Anyway I wouldn't make much money out of this lot!"

When they had finally shifted most of the boxes from one side of the room to the other, they found a small wooden packing crate. Initially they had some difficulty opening this, as nails still held the lid in place. But they gave it a heave and the lid finally came off. Inside, packed in tissue paper was a neatly folded pile of thick brown monks' habits.

"That'll do," said Charlie, feeling strongly that anything was better than those stockings.

They each pulled a pile out and went through into the house. Here they took it in turns to try them on. They were good ones, brown, and all had hoods that hung right over the face, "So nobody would recognize us," admitted Ivan.

"That's it," Archie agreed, "we can cover up whenever we want to be to be anonymous."

It was actually quite difficult to see where you were going with the hood in place. But, nonetheless, they managed to find the right sizes for the three of them and they seemed to be absolutely and exactly what they wanted.

Still hot from their efforts, they sat at the kitchen table and finished off a large tub of Hockings ice cream Ivan had brought the week before from the van in Torrington.

"They will do the trick. Frighten the life out of the buggers," Archie grinned.

"Should do," Ivan agreed. They retained a costume each, and Ivan replaced the others in the old box. He put the lid back on and they locked them back in the storage room.

"So when are we going to do it?" asked Charlie.

And the other two thought about it for a moment.

"Well," Ivan postulated, "we can't choose a night when they are having parties."

Charlie responded, "They tend to have their parties at the weekends, people come down from London and that."

"That counts out Friday, Saturday and Sunday," Archie agreed, "probably Wednesday or Thursday then."

"We could do Monday," Ivan suggested, "because they will be so exhausted from the weekend they will sleep well."

"No," interjected Charlie, "They'll probably be so exhausted from the weekend that they won't wake no matter how much noise we make."

Eventually it was agreed that the event was to take place early the following Thursday morning. They were to enter the house at approximately one o'clock, and would frighten the living daylights out of the new residents of Mill House.

Chapter 10

Maureen was extremely unhappy. She was wet, cold, and singularly bad
tempered. For three whole hours she had been sitting under a hedge watching
the farmhouse. The grass was wet, and the damp had permeated through the
blanket to her legs, and she was having some difficulty keeping them awake.
All the while the three fools within laughed about costumes, if she hadn't been
so good natured, she might have set fire to the bloody place while they were in
there. She could have done with the warmth. First they had laughed about one
costume, and then they had gone hunting for others. What the hell were they
for she wanted to know? She could gather from what she had overheard
through the headphones that the first costume had been a Quaker outfit. That
was where the stockings had come into it. The second outfit she wasn't entirely
sure. But again there had been much laughter and discussion of hoods. The
equipment worked some of the time, but occasionally there would be a lot of
static, and clicking noises, when for some reason, the signal had been
interrupted. So she was only able to pick up one conversation in three.
She understood they were going somewhere, and that there were costumes
involved, but had no idea where. Eventually two figures emerged from Greenly
Barton, and in their respective vehicles, made their way up the drive. She
repacked the blanket, and started on the long bicycle ride back to the village.
She made her way home slowly, still wet and cold, and dark thoughts coursed
through her veins as she struggled up the hill. They ranged from plans to cut
Ivan's break cables to burning his house down. Maybe anonymous letters might
do it or some juicy slander for the hairdressers, or something stimulatingly
libelous for the Church notice board.
But the possibility of being caught worried her. Every window had its net
curtain, and behind every curtain was someone who should have minded their
own business. The trouble with Devon, Maureen thought as she struggled up
the last hundred yards, was that it was a county full of curtain twitchers.
They didn't behave like that in Coventry. In Coventry they knew how to behave
and watched their televisions like good respectable people instead of spying on
their neighbors.
By the time she reached the house, she was in an extremely bad temper. Charlie
was already in front of the television with his feet up. She went straight upstairs
for a bath - and to hide the equipment.
When she came down she was in a slightly better frame of mind. But when he
asked about supper, her temper seemed to boil again.
"I'm not just your bloody servant," she said, going through into the kitchen.
"You can cook your own bloody supper!" he heard from within.
He contemplated going into the village and getting some fish and chips, and
initially thought better of it. "There must be something in the fridge," he
thought to himself, but the noises from within, Aunt Agatha like boomings,
dissuaded him from looking.
So while she was making something for herself he crept out. He ate his fish and

chips sitting on a bench in the High Street, and had a pleasant conversation with a couple of pensioners who were also enjoying a fish supper. When he got home, it was to find she had already gone up to bed. He slipped into his own room, taking care not to wake her. The next morning her temper had improved marginally. She made him a cup of tea, and asked him about his plans for the coming week. It was then that he mooted that he might be going up to Bude on Wednesday evening to do a bit of sea angling. "Who are you going with?" she asked.

"Oh it's a chap I know who lives up there," he said.

"Who's that?" she asked.

"Jim McKay," he lied, "I met him years ago he was working for a cement company. He's very into sea angling and has offered me a rod."

She went through to the kitchen contemplating this piece of news. If he was out on Wednesday night that was when he was going to be up to whatever it was - with the other two and the costumes. "Well whatever it is," she said to herself, "it's all going to center around Ivan's house."

And so when shortly after eight the following Wednesday evening he said good night and disappeared, she was ready. She put on a thick parker over a warm jersey, good waterproof trousers and gumboots. She bicycled down through the village with a couple of blankets and the equipment strapped to the pillion, and headed for Greenly Barton.

Taking the back lane rather than approaching on the main drive, she secreted herself and the bicycle in the hedge near the house. She had already inserted new batteries, and the equipment seemed to be working quite well on this occasion. She could hear them discussing costumes, timings, and so on. Mention was also made of beer and pop groups, but then the stutter began again and all was silent for a while.

Then the transmitter came to life again and she could hear the three laughing and drinking, "Have another," she heard someone say.

"I've had three already."

"Go on, it'll do you good."

"Have you set the alarm?"

"That's your job," she heard her husband say.

Eventually she settled down to a cold wet night in the hedge. Later she heard her husband seeming to remove his shirt and get into bed, or at least that's what it sounded like.

"Very strange," she thought, "I expected them to be out and about doing something," but there didn't seem to be any indication of that.

The lights in the house went out, and she sat shivering in the hedge despite the layers.

"Well," she thought, "if I've got to go through this I'm going to damn well have Ivan in jail before tomorrow night."

Fortunately it didn't rain, but it was turning out to be a very cold night. She must have woken twenty five times with the cold and damp seeping through her clothes to her skin. Even with all the extra layers to keep warm, it seemed to get to the marrow of her bones quicker than she ever expected. She shivered so violently that her teeth began chattering. Once or twice she had to get up and do jumping exercises in an attempt to try and stay warm.

At some point in the early morning, lights came on, so she sat and turned the equipment back on. She heard noises, but no conversation, grunts, clatter of teacups, and scraping of chairs. Eventually she saw the three figures emerge from the house and lock the door behind them. In the dim moonlight she saw shadows pile into Ivan's van carrying bundles. The car started, and disappeared up the drive.

In the dim moonlight she watched the car headlights, and scrambled up a small tree to try and see which direction they went. She saw the van reach the lane, turn left, continue on up the hill, and then branch left again. It then came down into the valley, passing the far end of the green lane she had followed, past Archie's house, and up the other side. Dimly she thought she saw it turn left again by the photographer's house in the far distance, suggested by a dim glow in the upper branches of the woods.

Uncertain as to where she was going, she packed the blankets and receiving equipment and got back on the bicycle. She headed back down the green lane towards Archie's house, and although it was somewhat soggy under her wheels she made good time. She passed Archie's house, dark and silent in the early morning dimness, only an owl noted her passing, and then branched left over the bridge.

It was hard work ascending the hill on the other side of the stream, but the exercise warmed her and drove out some of the chill. In a field next the lane a herd of cows made mooing noises at her. At the top of the slope she got her bearings. There was a fork in the road ahead, the left turn lead on down towards the river where there had once been a ford, she supposed. The right fork went off towards the three bridges, and then up the other side to the Bealand road. The drive to Mill House came off at a left hand fork. She wondered if that was where they were going. So she coasted downhill on the bicycle, narrowly missing a badger on route, and made her way to the entrance to Mill House. Leaving the bicycle in a bush by the gate, she walked up the drive towards the house. There were no lights, and the house was silent. Neither was there any sign of Ivan's van.

Well if they hadn't come this way, she thought to herself, they must have gone the other way. She retraced her steps, retrieved the bicycle, and followed the right hand fork towards the three bridges, which was where she found the van. It was parked in front of a gateway, about 50 yards from the first bridge. She regretted now that she hadn't brought a torch, as it was now extremely difficult to see where she was going. There was a new moon, shining palely through the clouds, but hardly enough to light her path in the thick woods. She certainly couldn't see enough to be able to recognize any footprints. She tried the front doors, hoping that there might be a torch inside. But both were locked.

She went round to the back and gave a good tug on the rear doors. At that point the catch broke, and with a snap the doors flew open. Something leapt out and disappeared into the night. Maureen peered into the back of the van, but could make out very little. There was a musty dog smell, so she guessed it must have been the dog that had jumped out. She promptly forgot about it, and opened the gate, and started following the muddy path up through the wood.

After she had gone about a hundred yards, it became so dark that she couldn't see where she was going, and the ground was boggy and treacherous. They were up to something, she was sure of it and it had something to do with Mill House. Briefly she wondered what life would be like if she didn't have to follow her husband about all night, sleeping in hedges and freezing half to death. She could have married a nice boring little man who played golf and followed the cricket. Somewhere in the back of her mind a quiet little voice said how dull it would have been.

But Maureen wasn't the sort of woman to listen to quiet little voices. She strongly suspected the hearts of golf playing and cricket loving husbands harbored dark fantasies about wetsuits and fishnet tights. It might have meant nights in far less pleasant places than hedges, and cold might not have been the only discomfort.

In the end she gave up following the muddy trail up the hill, and decided that instead that she would stake out Mill House. Just in case she could see anything going on through the windows. She re-traced her steps round to the front of the House, hid the bicycle and planted herself in a nice dry rhododendron bush, with a good view of the house and waited.

Chapter 11

Archie had led the way, and each man carried a bag containing his monk's habit. He took them into the crevice, and replaced some of the branches behind them, just in case they were followed.

"Now keep it down," he whispered forcefully, and they edged their way silently into the cavern, torches in hand. When they reached the far end Archie could see the back of the cupboard in place as before.

"Now," Archie whispered, "we've got to push it t'one side. Gi me a'and."

He stuck himself down on the ground as he'd done previously, and pushed hard with his feet. The other two pushed gently from above and it slid silently out of their way. It left a good gap of about a foot and a half that they could squeeze through. They removed their boots, and left them inside the tunnel. Then they opened the bags and donned the habits.

They proceeded gingerly, on tiptoe, toward the door of the scullery. Archie preceded them and, as before, he lifted the latch silently and peered down the corridor.

The house was silent, and only the ticking of a clock somewhere in the distance disturbed the sepulchral stillness.

"Let's have a look round first," Ivan whispered, "just in case there's anybody about."

They turned right out of the scullery, leaving the door slightly ajar, and made their way down the corridor, past the kitchens and into the great hall. The bear was still there, glowering menacingly in the dim light.

Charlie, who'd not been inside the house before, walked backwards looking up in case there were any signs of activity from the floor above. He was worried that with their late night parties, they might still be upstairs doing what ever pop musicians did in the early hours of the morning. He backed into something soft and looking up to see what had arrested his progress found an enormous muzzle snarling down at him.

For a brief moment he froze. Then his legs released their hold on the ground and he flew across the great hall and on to the table at the far end.

The other two men were taken by surprise not just by his rapid movement, but by the odd scream he made as he fled.

They looked about bewildered, and then stifled laughter when they realized what had initiated his action.

Charlie, seeing the stuffed bear for what it was, came down from the table with a red face only mildly hidden by the dim light.

"For God's sake keep it down," Ivan whispered.

"Sorry," Charlie replied.

They crept silently through the rooms on the ground floor of the house.

Through the drawing room, dining room, hall, and smoking room, but all was silent. Nobody was awake.

"Let's go and have a look at the old Mill room," whispered Archie, and he led the way down some steps. It wasn't what any of the three had expected at all; for they had anticipated a great big room stuffed full of old furniture, and perhaps a few pictures. It had been used as a storage room. Not a bit of it this time. There was a most curious conservatory like construction against the far wall.

"What the hell's that?" whispered Ivan.

"No idea!" Archie replied.

"Very strange." agreed Charlie.

They peered closely at it but could make out very little. In the dark they could see furniture within, but resisted the temptation to open the door. On one side of the room, was a cupboard.

"Have a look at this," whispered Archie, and opened the door silently. They examined the bottles within. They appeared to contain some white powdery substance, although one or two were a strange greenish colour.

Suddenly something exploded at them out of the dark and frightened the life out of all three of them.

"Bloody Hell!" Ivan exclaimed when he regained his breath.

"For God sake Pitch how the hell did you get in here?"

The dog wagged its tail happily.

Charlie picked himself up from the floor on the far side of the room.

Being frightened nearly out of his skin twice in one evening was beginning to play on his nerves. An evening with Maureen and her relatives was just slightly less frightening, and generally he had more time to steel himself beforehand. He was beginning to regret being enticed into the escapade, and wondered if he shouldn't have found some excuse and kept out of it.

"We've dropped some of the bottles," Ivan whispered kneeling down. He began to tidy up the white powder on the floor. It was a bit of a mess, not only had two small vials been smashed, but a bottle had been dropped as well.

As he was attempting to do this, Charlie knocked another bottle off the shelf with his elbow. It was very difficult to see what they were doing in the dim light. Then Archie reappeared, with a dustpan and brush.

"Just sort it out, for God's sake!"

Duly the white powder was dusted up and the bottles were refilled, appropriately or otherwise. The glass from the broken vials they wrapped in paper and stuffed into the pockets of Ivan's jacket. They then replaced the bottles on the shelves, pushing them back into position as best they could. Then closing the door, they made their way back up the steps of the Mill room, toward the Great Hall.

"Right then," said Archie, "I think we can start now." It had all been planned, they had even practiced it at Greenly Barton, and each man knew exactly what to do. So they crept to their appropriate positions and started the night's entertainment.

They began to moan and groan and gradually the most appalling noises started to echo through the old house.

At first it seemed there was to be no reaction to their efforts, so Charlie in the dining room, Archie in the drawing room and Ivan under the stairs in the great hall increased the volume of their moans. Ivan hung on to Pitch's collar and hoped to heaven the damn dog wouldn't get away again. He did consider heading back to the van, and locking Pitch in, but thought that if he did so he would be accused of dereliction of duty by the other two.

So he moaned as loud as he could, and as he did so, Pitch - perhaps not surprisingly, began to howl. This was a great game. And louder the three groaned and moaned, the louder Pitch howled.

Upstairs, Richard Fox was woken from a most excellent dream about his sister in law. He lay awake, listening to most odd yowling noises, not entirely sure if he was awake or not. In his bed in the dark he searched for a rational explanation for the extraordinary noises he was hearing.

He pinched himself to check if he was awake, and ascertained that he was. He wondered if somebody had caught a cat or something. Eventually, with the noise failing to quieten, but rather increasing in volume, he climbed out of his bed, turned the light on, and with a hand shading his eyes, made his way along the landing toward the stairs.

He met a couple of others milling about on the landing, as perplexed as he was. "What the hell is it?" asked Shamus.

"I've got no bloody idea, why are you asking me?" retorted Fox.

"I think an animal has got into the house," the other man said.

"Don't be bloody stupid;" said Fox, "all the doors are locked."

Downstairs the three men heard signs of activity. They continued their racket with gusto. Archie headed through the dark rooms and joined the other two, who had assembled shortly before in the hall. Ivan made movements with his thumb towards the kitchen and the three, gradually reducing the volume of their output, crept back towards the scullery.

It was at that point that a light on the landing appeared, and they saw Richard Fox siluetted above them in his red silk pajamas. It was then that Pitch made her bid for freedom. Howling like a banshee, she was up the stairs, and after Fox before anybody had a chance to do anything.

Fox was leaning over the banister, trying to see what the hell was going on below, when something bit him extremely painfully on the backside. He screamed loudly, managed to prevent himself flying into the stairwell, and fled back down the corridor. Shamus and Shaun, who had been standing beside him, also fled back to their own rooms and slammed their doors behind them.

Fox wasn't quite quick enough, once inside he attempted to close the door to his bedroom, but was out maneuvered by the speed with which Pitch could move when she wanted to. She got her fangs into his ankle twice, once into his calf, and then into the other buttock, by which time; Richard Fox was making more noise than the three men downstairs put together.

He tried to get back into the corridor, but was beaten to the door by the dog. Eventually, he managed to get into the wardrobe at the end of the bed and shut the door rapidly behind himself. With the wonderful red pajamas gone from her field of vision, Pitch gave up the chase, and headed back down the stairs to rejoin her master. They were waiting for her in the scullery, and she appeared tail wagging and with a scrap of red silk still in her mouth. Archie closed the scullery door and the three figures entered the cleft and pulled the cupboard back into place.

"Bloody dog!" complained Ivan as they made their way back through the cave and into the open air.

Maureen, who had been sitting cold and uncomfortable in the rhododendrons, had heard the noises in the house and, although somewhat mystified, was fairly sure it was something to do with Ivan. She hurriedly emerged from the shrubbery, and made her way down the lane to a phone box. She put a ten pence piece in the slot and phoned the police in Torrington.

"It's a burglary," she told the operator.

"Where?" asked the constable on duty.

"Mill House, near Somleigh," she hissed.

"Are you in the house?" he asked.

"No,"

"Where are you then?"

"In a phone box,"

"What's your name?"

"Can't tell you that," she said.

"Why not?" he asked.

"I was just passing, and saw someone breaking in, but it's nothing to do with me. You have to get here quickly."

"They'll phone you themselves in a minute I expect," she added, "you had better get someone here sharpish." and she replaced the receiver.

Police Constables Jim Spicer and Sarah Bowden were sitting as usual in their car at Somleigh Beacon through the early hours of the morning. It was their practice to try to make the time pass by talking about anything that came into their heads.

They'd been on duty since nine o'clock the previous evening, and had only two call outs during that time. The first to a suspected heart attack; to wait for the ambulance; and the second to a pub throwing-out.

"Brown," argued Jim.

"No," Sarah responded, "definitely rainbow."

"I'm sure it's brown," Jim argued again.

"I was defiantly told rainbow,"

"Well I shall look forward to getting a rod whatever they've got," Jim said.

"Yes, but rainbows go better for the fly, so if they have rainbows it will be much better," continued Sarah.

They were both keen fishermen, and were much looking forward to the creation of a fly-fishing lake in the area. It had been discussed for some months now, as the planning permission had been given, and the digging was well under way.

Then the radio buzzed into life.

"Bidstable calling car 42, car 42, car 42."

Sarah took the microphone and held the button down.

"Car 42 over."

The voice at the other end of the microphone came through loud and clear, "We've had a report of a burglary at Mill House in Somleigh, do you know the place, over?"

Sarah looked at Jim and he shook his head. She pressed the switch again.

"No we don't, can you give us some directions, over."

The voice at the other end continued, "Hang on a minute," and there was the sound of maps being shuffled as he searched for appropriate directions.

"Found it," the voice said at last.

The sound of a map being flattened came through the radio.

"Ok," the voice continued, "through Somleigh, down past the Church, to the bottom of the hill, right over a bridge, about two miles and then next left. Down towards the river anyway, over."

"Thanks John," Sarah responded, "out."

Jim started the car and they headed down towards Somleigh. There was no point in putting the siren on at this time of morning; they only got complaints if they did. And there wasn't much traffic around at this time of day anyway.

It didn't take them many minutes to get through Somleigh, past the church and they were soon on their way down the hill. They passed Maureen hidden and unseen in a gateway with her bicycle. When they arrived at the old house, they were at first unsure as to whether they were at the right place or not, as although it had large gateposts, there was no sign of a nameplate. However the lights were on, so they drove up to the door and parked in amongst the cars by the entrance.

"Nice cars," said Jim, Sarah made no comment.

They went to the front door, well illuminated by the many lit windows. The first thing people generally did after a burglary was to turn all the lights on, so it seemed to Jim and Sarah that the report had been correct. Anyway, unless there had been a burglary, why would anyone be up at this time of the morning? Jim gave the knocker a couple of heavy thumps, and stood back to wait. Quickly, the door was opened, and a man in a dressing gown ushered them inside.

"Thanks for coming so quickly," he said with an American accent, and led them into the hall.

"We've had a report of a burglary Sir."

The man turned and looked confused. "Burglary, no, there's no burglary, but we've got a man attacked by a dog, come on up, you had better speak to him," and he led them up through the hall and up the stairs. They were escorted into one of the bedrooms where a man was lying naked from the waist down on a bed and another man was treating his wounded backside with cream and cotton wool. Sarah reverse tracked rapidly and waited outside, while Jim continued in. There were four or five men in the room, and the man on the bed looked exceedingly embarrassed about the whole thing.

"Invite a few more, why don't you?" he said disgruntled from the bed.

Jim, although confused, knew that his duty was to record as much as he could and as quickly as he could. He pulled his notebook from his pocket, fetched out a pencil, and proceeded to question the men in the room.

"I'm going to need an account of what happened here tonight," he said addressing himself to the American.

Mickel started to explain, "Well we were woken, by this howling, and came out of our rooms to see what was going on. When we got to the top of the stairs we could see dogs running about down below us in the hall. And one of them came up the stairs and attacked Richard here."

Next Jim addressed himself to the man treating the injured victim, "are you a doctor?"

"No," the man responded, "I'm a Chemist."

"Do you know what you're doing?"

"Think so, just sterilising the wounds."

"Ouch, take it easy."

"Is it serious? Does he need to be in hospital?" Jim asked.

"No, he'll be alright, I'm just got to bind it up and make sure it's clean."

"Ouch," complained the figure on the bed, "watch where you put that bloody cream."

"Ok, probably better to get him to a doctor tomorrow anyway," Jim said.

"No problem."

"So how did these dogs get in in the first place?" asked Jim.

"That's the strange bit, we don't know."

"What do you mean you don't know?"

"Well, all the doors and windows were locked as far as we can see, but a whole pack of them got in! They were making enough noise to wake the dead."

"How many dogs did you see?"

"How many did you see?" Mickel asked the other members of the group. One of them confirmed that he'd seen the one that had come up the stairs. Others said they'd seen five or six others rushing about below them in the hallway. Jim wrote it all down carefully in the notebook. He then recorded the names of the people involved. Finally they returned to the ground floor. When they reached the hall they were given a guided tour, and took the opportunity of checking the doors and windows. As they had said, they were all securely locked.

As they left by the front door, he addressed himself to Mickel again.

"I don't see what we can do, at this stage, but if you find out anything else please let us know as quickly as you can."

"Sure," responded Mickel, "but do me a favour, please don't spread it about." Jim said they would do what they could, and the two figures disappeared into the night. On their way back to the Beacon in the squad car, they discussed the night's events.

"That man was obviously torn about a bit," Jim said.

"Did you see how his legs were lacerated"?

"Yes," agreed Sarah. "I was only in the room for a second, but I could see he was quite badly cut."

"Absolutely," Jim confirmed, "but this dog story is very queer indeed."

"Do you think they are covering up for something else," Sarah asked.

"I don't really know," Jim said. "There could be something very odd going on there, there could have been a fight or something, and they made this story up to hide the facts. And who was the woman that phoned it in?"

"No idea, unless she let the dogs in." said Jim.

"Did you see any women in the house?"

"No,"

"No, nor did I," agreed Jim.

"Even stranger," agreed Sarah.

And within ten minutes they were back at the Beacon where Sarah radioed in their report, and they waited for their end of shift at four o'clock that morning. With a couple of hours to kill, Jim decided to catch forty winks, and Sarah was left listening to his heavy breathing and wondering about the events at Mill House.

There were lots of explanations to what they had seen, but packs of dogs breaking and entering wasn't one of them. Her thoughts ranged from wild parties, to sadism, to drugs and on to punishment beatings. But all the while the fact that a woman had rung in the burglary report, blew all her theories out of the water. Perhaps they were running a white slave ring, recruiting local girls and selling them to the Middle East.

She wondered if they would let her go undercover. But it might be dangerous. After all she might end up as an Arab's sheik's concubine, sleeping on black silk sheets, and wearing nothing but gold and precious stones. On reflection that sounded an awful lot more exciting than listening to Jim snoring at 3.30 in the morning, and she decided to volunteer.

Hugh Sweeting, lay in his bed and listened to the police report on the radio. He was an insomniac and had been for over twenty years; two hours of sleep a night was his average. The long hours seemed to drift by slowly, but over the years he developed the habit of having the radio on, which sometimes helped. As time had gone on, he'd become bored with the local radio stations and their inane chatter. So he'd tried radio 4, but that had kept him awake. Then he tried radio 3, but he didn't really like classical music, and Radio 2 had the same effect as 4. In the end discovered the police frequencies quite by chance one night. He heard the first call that night, and had listened to it with interest.

A burglary at Mill House. How very interesting he thought to himself. There was the odd burglary in the area, but it was generally teenagers after a bit of loose cash. This however sounded like a professional job.

Later he heard a call coming through for the same car, but it didn't respond. He presumed the police were already inside Mill House interviewing people. Later still he heard them filing a report about dogs and he lay awake through the early hours wondering about this.

When he went down to the village shop that morning to buy his copy of the Western Morning News he repeated the story.

In the newsagent they didn't believe a word of it. In the bakers they were sceptical. In the butchers they thought it possible, but unlikely, but in the grocers he was told about it by the assistant. So by lunchtime the whole village knew.

Chapter 12

The three men re-traced their steps back to three bridges, took the van with Charlie and Pitch in the back, and headed straight back to Greenly Barton. Ivan and Archie sitting in the front discussed the chances of their night's work having the desired effect.

"That bliddy dug of yourn hasn't helped matters," said Archie.

"Well err, sorry about that, didn't know that was going to happen, she was supposed to be well locked up in the back," apologised Ivan, "I've no idea how she got out."

"We'll have to keep it prapper quiet though," Archie said.

"If it gets out that it was us," he continued "we'll have the police down on us like a ton of bricks. And you'll have your dog taken away as well."

Ivan hadn't thought of that.

As they drove up the drive to the house, they could hear Piggy Roberts calling his cows in for milking on the other side of the valley.

"Get your bloody asses up here you stupid heaps of manure!" he yelled.

Ivan wondered why they came at all, as he always used such rich language. And why was he called 'Piggy'? He didn't even keep pigs!

Later they sat around the kitchen table in Greenly Barton, and drank tea liberally dosed with whisky. Then they retired to their beds.

It was after 11 o'clock the next morning that they finished a good fried breakfast and headed out. Ivan needed milk, bread and a newspaper, and followed them toward the village. While he was queuing with three pensioners to buy his paper, he listened in on their conversation.

"Oh yes," one old woman said to another, "and a man was bitten by them. He's took bad. And my cousin says they have been killing sheep for weeks, and the police are hunting for them and have offered a reward, and they're going to call in professional hunters."

"I heard they weren't dogs," responded the other woman, "my brother was told by Major Stanley that they were wolves. He said the prints were all wrong for dogs."

"First wild cats, now wolves."

"Yes, I think we'll have to be careful where we go now."

"What's all this?" asked Ivan.

"Oh hello Ivan, I didn't see you there," she said, "how's you?"

He confirmed that he was hale and hearty.

"So what's this about dogs?"

"Well," they said, "it's all over, everybody is talking about it, somebody got attacked by a pack of dogs last night."

"Who?" Ivan asked.

"Some chap down near the river."

"Oh that's nothing," the newsagent said, "I heard there was a chap bitten last week over in Hatherley."

It was a fairly common occurrence in the area, most people kept a dog of one sort or another.

"Yes," confirmed another old woman, "t's different though; a whole pack got into the house and attacked the people."

"Where's this then?" he asked.

"Oh, down Mill House."

"What, the new people there?"

"That's right."

"Do they keep dogs?" the newsagent asked.

"No, don't think so."

"So how did they get in?"

"I don't know my dear, maybe they left a door open or something."

"Was he killed?" Ivan asked, suddenly worried.

"No don't think so, just bitten a bit," she said.

"So what are the police going to do about it?" Ivan asked.

"Don't know, but I hear they've got marksmen out hunting for them, and there's a reward as well."

"Very mysterious," Ivan said, deciding that it would be a good idea to keep Pitch on a lead for a day or two.

"Yes, t'is that my dear," said the old woman.

When he got to the butchers there was a debate going on there as well.

"Not dugs, wolves' great big hairy things,"

"Escaped from Bideford zoo," someone said.

"Don't be daft, it has to be dogs!"

"Can't be wolves, the zoo closed last year," somebody else contradicted.

"They might have been mastiffs not wolves; we don't get any wolves around here."

"Maybe they let them go on the moor, like they did with big cats a few years back."

He didn't stay to hear the rest of the debate, but later when he got home the phone rang, it was Charlie from the village phone box.

"Do you hear what they're saying?" he said.

"Yes," Ivan said.

"Talking about wolves and dogs and stuff. That Pitch of yours has upset the apple cart no end."

"They should have been talking about ghosts," Ivan grumbled.

"Not a bit of it," Charlie said. "They're convinced themselves there was a pack of dogs or wolves or some other nonsense. People are right frightened now, even the Vicar. He says he's not going out on his bicycle, and will only use his car from now on."

"It's not at all what we planned." said Ivan.

"No, it's not, instead of frightening them out, they're likely to just lock themselves in and refuse to come out at all." confirmed Charlie.

"How's that going to help us?" asked Ivan.

"Not sure it will," Charlie agreed. "But we'll see, I've got to get down there this afternoon. Got some work to do. I'll see what's up.

When he arrived there just before 1 o'clock, he was met at the gate by a seven foot Neanderthal in jeans and a tee shirt.

"What you want?" the man grunted.

"I'm the gardener," Charlie explained, keeping it short, doubting the man's reasoning skills, and keeping well clear of the pickaxe handle he was swinging about.

"Name?"

Charlie told him.

"Oh, right," he pulled a sheet of paper from a pocket and studied it, "you'd better go in then."

Charlie went on in, and got on with what he had to do, and nobody seemed to take any notice of him. Later, he caught a glimpse of the over-grown majorette throwing his pick axe handle in the air, and dropping it.

A little bit of light mowing, backwards and forwards across the lawn, eventually a window opened and somebody shouted at him. He turned the mower off and approached the window.

"Can I help you?" he asked. He didn't recognize the man; but thought he must be one of the Cordaxe musicians.

"Have you seen any dogs?" the man asked.

"Sorry sir?"

"Yes there's a pack of dogs roaming around, they're vicious."

"I'll keep my eyes open then," said Charlie.

"Yes, you watch yourself mate," said the voice from within, "they're big, and dangerous too." Then the window slammed closed.

Trying hard to look as mystified as possible, Charlie stood and scratched his head. After a moment or two he returned to his mowing. During the afternoon there was little sign of life from the house. They had locked themselves in and weren't coming out for anything. Later Dr Hughes turned up, and was allowed through by the Neanderthal. He stayed for about twenty minutes, and drove off again.

The next day the Western Morning News had a bit on it, and they pored over the article in the bar that evening.

"Doesn't say much do it?" said Archie.

"No." agreed the other two.

A packs of dogs, reported to be roaming wild in the Somleigh area it said. It advised local residents to keep doors and windows closed, and to not go out alone. The police were baffled, but had said they were waiting further developments and were looking into the matter.

They did however deny that they had marksmen out and refuted there being a reward.

"Means they ha't got a bloody clue," Archie said.

"Best thing," agreed Ivan.

"Well Pitch did get that man Fox," said Archie, "shame she didn't kill the buggar."

"Did you see how fast he moved with Pitch after him?" asked Ivan.

"Yes, that were good, like the red Indian, knee-high the son of gym-shoe," joked Archie. "Worst thing is, what with everybody talking about it, its beginning to get to me. I keep finding myself locking windows and doors and going out with a big stick."

"I did something like it this morning," said Ivan, "it starts to get to you after a while,"

"So what are we going to do now?" asked Charlie.

"Do?" asked Ivan.

"Well we've got to do something else; our first attempt hasn't worked has it?"

"I suppose not," said Ivan.

"Look at it this way, we wanted them out, but now they've dug themselves in and battened down the hatches. If I have to carry on drinking this muck for the next few years, I don't think I'll bother coming to the Oak any more," said Charlie, looking unhappily at his cider.

"I'll think about it bit," said Archie, "mayhap be I'll think of something."

Chapter 13

Over the next few days, Archie mulled the situation over. He was out and about as usual, even though one or two people said he was foolish to be on his own with a pack of dogs on the loose. Even the local hunt was called off that weekend.

"Until the matter is clarified," explained the Master.

Charlie carried on with his gardening as normal. Ivan returned to the essential tasks of running a small farm, while Archie took to wandering around the fields and woods around Mill House. Occasionally he got himself a pheasant or a rabbit. But he had a puzzle to solve. What else could they do to get rid of the buggers. Couldn't burn the place down, that was too drastic and probably see the three of them in prison and possibly people dead. But there must be some way.

On the Saturday, more cars appeared, and he watched from the hill above the house as they prepared for another party. They had a couple of heavies wandering around on the drive clutching their pickaxe handles. And there seemed to be more activity in the house than out.

No marquees this time, or trestle tables on the lawns. As he sat on a tree stump, behind a holly bush, his eyes wandered down towards the river. The warmer weather had dried out some of the grass, which was beginning to look a little bit yellowed. He could clearly see a line stretching across the lawn, revealing the course of the culvert, which had originally supplied water to the mill wheel. He followed it with his eyes through the rhododendron border and across a field. In the field it wasn't just a dip, but a fully-fledged channel, or leat. Now empty of course, seemingly clogged by weeds and brambles.

The next day, he decided to have a look at this leat. He approached it from the river end. The river was slightly lower than normal, and he could easily see where the leat had been walled off from the main course of the river. The wall was solidly made of rounded river stones and cement. It must have been built when the house had been converted from a mill. Probably sixty or seventy years ago, back near the turn of the century, he imagined. He could see that even with the river at its present level, if the wall had not been there, the water would have flowed freely down the leat towards the house.

Archie followed the leat across the field. It was heavily clogged with brambles, stinging nettles and elder. He was screened from the house by the rhododendrons, and was therefore not worried about observation. Once nearer the rhododendron screen, the leat ended, and the drain began. He clambered down an elder tree into the channel. It was about four feet deep at that point and with his elderly legs it took some doing. But once down, he could see the mouth of a large drain, coming out from under the rhododendrons. It must have been about a foot and a half wide. He took his knife out, and whittled a long piece of elder stem into a sharp spar. Then he pushed it into the drain to see how far it would go. It went in about nine feet, and there was no sign of any obstruction.

He mused to himself; 'perhaps the thing's still open after all this time'. He peered down it again, and wished he had a torch. He grinned as a plan came into his head.

Later, he walked back up the hill overlooking Mill House and took his customary seat on the tree stump. He was sure the drain ran under the lawn, and would originally have joined the millpond. On one side of the fish pond there was a stone balustrade, and he presumed this was where the water had been channeled to hit the mill wheel. Down below, there was another patio, and French windows leading out of the Mill room. They must be new, he said to himself. Originally, that would be part of the channel. He decided to ask Charlie to tell him more about it, and when they met in the pub that evening he questioned him closely.

"So what's on the far side of the balustrade," he asked.

"Well there's a nine foot wall," Charlie confirmed, "and then there's a small patio with statues and pot plants and stuff."

"Is there any sign of where the mill wheel was?" asked Archie.

"No, but there's a hole in the wall with bricks in it so you can see where it came out, but there's no sign of any channel or anything."

"Isn't there a drain from the pond or anything?" asked Ivan, beginning to understand where Archie's thoughts were leading.

"No there's no sign of anything like that, it's all much newer I think."

Eventually after much conjecture Archie, under his breath, so as not to be overheard, asked the other two, "So, what would happen, if the river were to get into the mill race again?"

"Into the leat?" asked Ivan, "depends on the drop of course, but I guess the river must be a good nine feet above the pond."

Charlie looked perplexed for a second and then the light dawned. "If it got through the leat," he conjectured, "and the drain under the lawn is still open, it would probably break through into the fishpond, and then come straight over by the balustrade."

"And then?" asked Archie.

"Oh then…" he remained silent for a few seconds. "It would all end up on the lower patio."

"And then?" coaxed Archie.

"It will go all over the place I guess, some of it would go onto the lawns, some of it would go… ah," he said, "into the Mill room."

He'd got it at last.

"Is the floor of the Mill room lower than the patio?"

Charlie admitted he wasn't sure.

"Well, when you go along tomorrow have a damn good look will you," said Archie.

The following day he spent some time down on the lower patio. A quick glance into the Mill room told him there was nobody about, and the lights were out. There was just enough light to be able to see that the floor was a foot lower. If the water got in, it would flood the whole room.

That night he met them in the bar as normal, and told them what he'd seen.

"So if the water gets down there, it'll flood the whole of the Mill room."

"Not enough to get them out of the house completely," Ivan said.

"Yes," agreed Archie, "but certainly enough to annoy em. They'll have builders in for the next three months trying to fix it."

"So how's it going to help us?" asked Charlie.

"Well the more problems we can cause them, the more likely they are to decide to move somewhere else, and hopefully take Richard Fox with them," Ivan said.

"Ok," the other two agreed.

"The tricky bit," Archie consolidated, "is shifting that wall. It's about a foot thick. And it's very solid."

"If I stick the front end loader on the tractor," Ivan said, "I should be able to fix it, just hit it a few times good square in the middle, that should do the trick."

Archie disagreed, "No, you will just break the buggar, got to hit it better than that. What you need," he said. "Is one of those pneumatic things, you know like

62

they use for digging roads."

"Yes that would certainly work, but it would make one hell of a din. And somebody is bound to come and have a look and see what all the noise is about."

"I hadn't thought of that," said Archie.

"Maybe you could stick a spike of some sort on the front of the tractor," Charlie suggested, "that's what we used to do when we were breaking ground for a motorway. If you came across something solid you couldn't shift, you just stuck a bloody great steel spike on the front of something big and just drove into it in low gear."

"Might work," agreed Ivan, "I'll have a look round, see what I can find."

And the next day he spent some time seeing what he could do with the tractor. He couldn't find a spike as such, but he found the remains of a girder, a four-foot bit left over from something or other. And he was able with some effort to bolt this on to the back of the tractor. They agreed on the telephone, that they would have a go, the following Friday night.

"Why Friday?" asked Charlie.

"Well they have parties on the Saturday and if we can get them to flood out right in the middle of a party, it will annoy them more than anything else we can do." So the plan was hatched, Ivan was to drive the tractor from Greenly Barton, Archie was to open the gates, and Charlie was to keep a watch in case of spectators.

On the Friday, in the dark of the late evening, Ivan drove the tractor, spike attached, through the quiet lanes down to the gate. Archie was there to meet him and let him through without any fuss. While Archie followed Ivan down to the river, Charlie stayed near the lane, and kept an eye out just in case. They worked together, Ivan reversing the tractor, and Archie guiding him.

He had to drive into the river which was about two feet deep at one point. But it turned out to be a lot easier than they'd expected, and the wall broke up almost straight away. They parked the tractor back in the field, and fell to work shifting some of the larger stones. Half an hour later, there was enough of a channel to allow the water through, and it was soon deep enough to come over the boots of both men. They retreated back into the field.

"Should do the job," Ivan grinned with satisfaction, "cement was rotten!"

"Water's coming through already," Archie said.

They could see he was right.

The three men parted, left the leat to fill in its own time, and headed back to their homes.

The next day, cars arrived throughout the afternoon as on previous occasions. It was a big do, with producers down from London, a couple of guys from the States, as well as promoters and musicians from all over Europe. They'd fixed up the dining room, and various groups were doing sessions. There were young scantily clad women, shipped in from London; there was booze, and other things. It paid to keep the producers happy. And some of the radio DJs had also come.

Richard Fox, who had now recovered from his unpleasant experience, made everybody welcome, and played the perfect host. Of course they had tried to prevent the dog story getting out, but the laughter behind Richard's back and the bad jokes soon told them it was widely known. Richard, although offered places to sit by almost everyone he met, bore it with fortitude.

They had people in from Exeter to serve drinks, a chef had come down all the way from Paris, and security men prowled the grounds – in case of problems, canine or otherwise.

Fox was still noticeably shy of dogs, and preferring to be on the safe side, endeavored to prevent the guests going out onto the lawns. However they soon opened the patio doors and were out whether he liked it or not. But he bit his lip, and joined them.

At about eleven o'clock they started to hear odd noises, which at first they couldn't identify. It was an odd rumbling sound, and a few of the less inebriated guests commented on it. Someone mentioned it to Mickel, who went and told Richard about it. Richard went outside on to the patio and listened.

"I don't know," he said.

It sounded like a train in a distant tunnel, but somehow, it appeared to be closer than they expected, almost as if it was coming from the gardens. He couldn't figure it at all.

"Maybe it's got something to do with the plumbing," he said.

He knew that old houses often had complex networks of lead piping.

"Better get some plumbers in tomorrow," he said, and left it at that.

By one o'clock in the morning, the noise had changed to a steady thumping beat. Almost like a large two-stroke engine. Fox went out on the higher patio, leant over the balustrade and listened, but still couldn't identify the source.

Then one of the guests pointed to the pond.

"Look at that!" he said.

There were lots of small bubbles rising to the surface of the pond. Richard Fox could also see that mud and twigs and sticks and other debris were being brought up from the bottom. He was even more convinced that a call to a plumber would be needed the following day. Fortunately, there was no smell. So it was unlikely to be a breakdown in the sewerage system; that was a small mercy in itself.

As the noise got louder however, the guests came out on the patio to savor the entertainment. Eventually, with over fifty people on the upper patio, trestle tables were carried out and loaded with food and drink.

Soon there were very few people left in the house, as they had come to look at the bubbling pond. A heated debate was taking place as to the reason for the disturbance. One of the Americans reckoned it was methane.

"Yes I've seen it before," he said, "comes up from dead material under the ground, like at the bottom of a lake or pond."

No one disagreed with him; after all they worked in the music industry and weren't plumbers or sewerage engineers. At about 2 o'clock in the morning, the noise changed subtly, from a thumping beat that deafened out even the music coming from the Mill room, to rather a sudden and loud hiss. It stilled them to silence, and they held their breaths and listened to this change in pitch and tone. Suddenly, a geyser of filthy water erupted from the centre of the pond.

"Pretty bloody amazing entertainment," a drunken reveler laughed, and a topless young lady agreed with him as the water shot forty feet vertically into the air.

Then it came down, like heavy rain. Very muddy heavy rain, contaminated with slime and bits of twig and all sorts of other detritus.

The guests began a disorderly and rapid retreat into the house. Those on the upper patio found themselves caught in a crush, as those before became wedged, and those behind pushed all the harder to escape the foul deluge. They soon clogged its small entrance as they struggled to re-enter the house. However beneath the pond changes were afoot. The pressure of the backed up water in the leat, and the flow of the river, broke a stone slab, which had served as a cover for the old drain.

Several hundred tons of water at great pressure then forced a new channel, and the nature of the geyser changed once again.

The geyser suddenly changed its direction of fire, and shot the foul effluent straight at the struggling mass. Like a fire hose it sprayed straight at the door, and pushed the mud-drenched crowd back into the house. The riot that ensued was like a cross between Dante's inferno and the world mud wrestling championships. They were drenched, sodden, bruised and battered, and coated from head to foot with a thick layer of black gelatinous mud.

Richard Fox found himself lifted off his feet and thrown bodily down the corridor. He scrambled painfully to reach safety and pulled himself over struggling mud coated mass in his flight. His legs and backside were hurting again. A London DJ, in his struggle to escape knocked him off his feet again, and they fought for position amongst the filthy mass of arms and legs.

Mickel found himself face down in the mud, with a stripper from Barnsley sitting on his head. He said a few choice words, and when she failed to respond, bit her hard below the waist. She screamed, and moved just far enough for him to be able to come up for air.

This was no fun and a major panic had ensued. The remains of the food and drink were everywhere, and people were slipping around in the slime. Women in short skirts and non-existent tops were mud wrestling in a desperate struggle to get through the door. Men whose need was no less desperate, but who had size and strength on their side, kicked them in the faces in their struggle for life. Those on the lower patio were mystified by the events taking place above them. There was a bit of spray coming down from above, and they could hear a lot of very strange noises. They didn't mind a little bit of rain, even if it was slightly muddy and being fairly well inebriated they were not overly worried by the events above.

Standing with drinks in hand, they listened to the impending crisis above them. Then an odd cracking noise seemed to emanate from the wall and they peered at it mystified. Then without notice, the wall seemed to disintegrate, and an avalanche of stones and thick mud fell on them, and the remains of the stone balustrade followed it. It rapidly swept down over them breaking legs and arms. Some of the guests were swept away from the door and patio, on to the lawns beyond.

The screams and yells of pain, fear and shock were far louder than the noise coming from the upper patio. Chaos ensued as mud bathed figures leapt to and fro, attempting to avoid the rock and mire. The spray, which had been concentrated on the upper patio, was now directed at the lower, and those who had been unable to get through the upper patio door, were now washed down on to those below. The struggling figures fought desperately with each other for foothold and to keep their heads above the spreading slime.

For the second time in two weeks, desperate phone calls were made to the police. And Jim and Sarah, again on duty at the Beacon after a week on the day shift, were impelled to rush to the rescue at an even greater speed than before. "For God's sake get there quickly," the voice on the radio said, "it sounds like all hell is breaking loose. The river seems to be washing the house away, from what we can understand. We'll have other cars on their way shortly, as well as ambulances."

And they drove through the village at fifty miles an hour that night, losing the off-side wing mirror on a wall by the church.

When they got to the house, they realized that the radio message had been no exaggeration. They saw before them a scene of utter devastation, with cars slumped into a landslip which spread over the edge of the wall. A thick mat of black mud had deluged over half of the lawn, and people were still dragging themselves out of this and endeavoring to help each other.

Sarah put in a rapid call to the ambulance service. "Better send us three or four, everything you've got I'm afraid, the place is a total mess, don't know what's happened, possibly some sort of mud slide, but total devastation and on first sight at least twenty injured."

The front door was already open, and they rushed inside with their first aid kit, and began trying to restore order. Sarah and Jim knew a little bit about triage, and endeavored to practice this, walking wounded were taken to the drawing room, where they were given non-alcoholic drinks.

"No alcohol please," Sarah told a waiter who was trying to help, "just water or soft drinks," but she knew it was a bit late as that most of them seemed to be heavily intoxicated already. The more seriously injured were placed on cushions on the floor and on the table in the dining room. She counted eight with broken limbs and one man with a bad head wound who was mercifully unconscious. Twenty minutes later ambulances arrived and the paramedics took over from Jim, who went to help Sarah in the drawing room.

They cleaned people up and helped to restore order and morale rather than just treating wounds. There were lots of grazes of course, and a few nasty cuts and bruises, but fortunately nothing life threatening in the drawing room.

Now having seen most of the house, Sarah was beginning to be convinced they were not white slave traders, and as the crisis gradually came under control, she experienced a certain disappointment that she was not to be kidnapped and taken to Arabia as a concubine after all. She wondered if Thomas Cook did package tours.

Hugh Sweeting in his bedroom had listened to the messages buzzing backwards and forwards between Bidstable police and the various police cars with great interest.

Not waiting for the sun to rise, he phoned the Western Morning News and left a message for the editor. By nine o'clock there were three reporters outside Mill House. They were rudely re-buffed and told aggressively to 'bugger off' by a security man with his arm in a sling. So, after trying unsuccessfully to interview survivors, they followed the convoy of ambulances back toward Bidstable, where they found the accident and emergency department full of the wounded from Mill House. Interviews were taken aplenty.

Chapter 14

Cassandra de Gate was being kept waiting, and was becoming increasingly annoyed about it. He was supposed to of been there at nine o'clock, and it was already ten past. She'd been sitting in her cat suit for the last ten minutes waiting for the fool to turn up. He was one of her regulars and came once a month at nine o'clock on a Wednesday evening. She worked on the basis of an hour per session, with a ten minute gap between for a cup of tea and a cleanup. Fortunately he was her last client of the evening, but she still had to get home and they knew they were supposed to be on time.

She had made it a rule to always wear a mask with her clients. She'd recognized too many of them over the years after seeing them in the newspapers, and once or twice the television, and it had made her cautious.

Her one worry was that she might be recognized, and the story getting back to Somleigh. If that happened, she might well be socially ostracized, which could damage not only her reputation in the village, but the profitability of the pub as well. Not that the Oak could be said to be profitable just at the moment what with the beer fiasco.

She might even have to sell up and leave, which was something she didn't even want to contemplate. It was her home after all.

The suit had not been easy to find, but she had bought it in a specialist shop in Soho. It was made of latex, and was difficult to get on, but even more difficult to remove. It was warm in the winter, but could be rather hot and sweaty in the summer. As it was it left her legs and arms bare, and only just covered her breasts. In the winter she wore long black lace gloves, but her legs did tend to get rather cold at times.

Her customers did not come to her for sex. They could get that from any of the numerous prostitutes - who also had flats in similar back streets in similar towns. No, if they had wanted that, they could pay about £10 or £20, whereas she charged over £100 per hour for the therapy she offered. This suited her down to the ground as she was appalled by the thought that she might be mistaken for a common prostitute. She would have been very angry and insulted if any of her clients had made that mistake.

She advertised her extremely select services in a number of specialist subscription only publications. If a client had ever asked her for sex in addition to her standard services, she might have assumed he'd made an honest mistake in choice of service, and sent him to see one of the local pros', probably saving him a small fortune in the process. Fortunately however, none ever had.

Most of her regulars did everything they could to hide their identity from her, even going so far as to park well away from the flat, in case she noted their car numbers. Some even went to the extreme of not bringing their wallets with them, in case she identified them from a cheque book or a driver's license.

The flat itself was in a back street in Taunton, well away from the more respectable areas. The road was lined with fish & chip shops, pubs, second hand shops and newsagents. Parking was no problem and people used the area for recreation. The flat was anonymous, and situated as it was above a second hand furniture dealer, it aroused little curiosity.

Eventually the bell went downstairs and an apologetic voice said, "Sorry got caught in traffic." She let him in with the buzzer and as he came up the stairs she put the mask back on.

"You're late," she said.

"Sorry Maam," he said, "caught in traffic."

"That's no excuse, there will be a penalty to pay," she explained as she locked the door behind him.

"Yes Maam," he apologized. She had him drop his trousers and bend over the bed. She then gave him six of the best with a Sjambok.

She liked using the Sjambok; it was about three feet long, and really a cross between a cane and a whip. When she had first opened the clinic, she had used a whip, but whips had the unfortunate habit of knocking china off the mantelpieces and smashing sherry bottles. Then one of her clients - who had been on holiday to South Africa - had given her one as a present. She wore them out at a rate of about three or four a year, and had had to set up a standing order with a company in Johannesburg.

Roger had rather let the side down by having his face plastered all over the Western Morning News about six years before. And so when he'd started coming to her a couple of years later she had thought she recognized him. Eventually she remembered, and had found the paper in the Exeter library. She never let on of course - there were unspoken rules.

Masochism was a very strange area, but she got a certain perverse pleasure in inflicting the pain that these men insisted on receiving. She made it seven strokes for good measure.

"Right," she said when she was done, "you will have to pay a proper penalty for your lateness today."

"Yes Maam," he said, shivering with excitement.

"I have some homework for you."

Homework was almost always well received, because not only did it keep them on the very heights of excitement till their next appointment, and got them back without fail. Occasionally it helped in other ways as well.

Sometimes she had them find her new clients, tell her about a horse running in the gold cup, or even once or twice a little bit of light surveillance.

But on this occasion she had another little plan in store. Roger, she knew worked for Customs and Excise in Bristol. He was apparently quite high up there, Director Level or at least that was what the article had implied. And she guessed he had the power to investigate anybody he wanted to. He had right of search, as did his people, and they could go into any organization and remove files if they wanted to. All he needed was suspicion. At least that was what the newspaper article had said.

"Right," she said and gave him another quick tickle with the Sjambok.

He yelled owing to its unexpected nature.

"You have one month to finish a little task I have for you."

"Yes," he spluttered, catching his breath, "whatever you want."

She hit him again.

"Quiet!"

He remained silent.

"I want you to find out what you can about a man called Richard Fox and a company he owns called Foxtradic."

His analytical brain kicked in, and he wanted to ask why, and if she knew he worked for Customs & Excise, but he didn't dare, "See what you can find out," she said.

"The more you find out the better, if you do really well I might even give you a free session, otherwise there will be more penalties to pay," and hit him again.

She then removed the rest of his clothing and gave him a good beating; he needed to get his money's worth after all.

By the time he'd paid and left, he was quivering with excitement, and the homework she had given him would keep him busy for the full month. Every time he put pen to paper or discovered something new, the thrill would return.

As she made her way home to Somleigh that evening, Joanna, otherwise Cassandra de Gate or 'Castigate' was reasonably satisfied that Roger would come up with something useful.

It was her little hobby, on her Wednesday afternoons off; she would make her way to Taunton, where she rented the flat under the name of Cassandra de Filias and there ran the clinic and entertained gentlemen callers in unusual ways. She didn't really need to do it any more, although it had helped her in the early days. But it was fun and she enjoyed seeing men grovel on the floor like idiots, and it still amused her hugely, even after all this time.

However there was a serious side to the job, as these men needed help to control their un-natural urges, and she did her best to fill that role. Most were ex public school boys, and had been introduced to masochism by an obliging housemaster or friendly prefect.

She saw them as victims really, and if they wanted a normal home life, with a normal wife and normal children, they had to keep a good firewall in place between their private urges and their family life. If the two got mixed up it tended to lead rapidly to divorce and unhappiness, and it was the job of her clinic to prevent this. The odd thing was that she seemed to need it just as much as they did. It was strange and she had no idea why, so in a way it was as much therapy for her as it was for them.

She remembered an episode with a potential lover when she had been a teenager. She had been laying on a hay bale in the loft above the barn, and he'd come to her, wearing only his socks and a smile. His mistake had been in removing his spectacles as well, as he had taken the open hatch for a tarpaulin, and had stepped on it and disappeared dramatically from view.

She had run to the hatch and found him crouching embarrassed on a pile of straw with all the cows trying to lick him. Then she had laughed till her sides hurt, and was still laughing. Perhaps that was it.

The biggest problem had been secrecy. It had increasingly been praying on her mind. Perhaps she ought to give it up, maybe by Christmas she could finish it all. But she was conscious she had been telling herself exactly the same for at least four years.

With these thoughts rattling around inside her head, she got back to Somleigh at quarter past eleven and let herself into the back of the bar just after chucking out time.

Chapter 15

A couple of days after the catastrophe the police and the insurers engaged a Quantity Surveyor from Exeter, who also happened to have a certain expertise in sewerage systems. He was well known in the area, being of aristocratic blood, and having a grand title. And he let everybody know it. He'd been commissioned to try and assess the cause of the landslip at Mill House, and had been asked to arrive at about three o'clock in the afternoon. He drove through the gates on the dot of three and was stopped by a man with a pickaxe handle. "Get out of my bloody way!" he shouted, leaning out of the car window, "I'm here to do the survey," and drove straight at the man.

The security guard leapt to one side and looked after him thinking dark thoughts about posh bastards and pick axe handles.

He climbed out of the Jaguar by the front door, extracted a pair of Wellingtons from the boot and put them on. He looked suitably professional, with three-piece suit, bow-tie and gumboots, allowing him to do the work, as well as looking somewhat like a pessimistic gynecologist. In order to charge the police the exorbitant fee he had in mind, he felt it only right to dress the part, and had a carnation in his buttonhole for good measure. He hammered the knocker against the oak door and waited.

The door opened and he introduced himself and marched in. Under his arm he carried the plans and notebooks. A young police constable was waiting for him inside.

"Hello Sir," he said. "I'm here to try and make sure that everything that you need is available to you."

"Good," he muttered, and marched on through, "where's the cellar?"

He was taken down the steps and was able to inspect some of the piping that led from the sewerage system. Behind him the young policeman asked irrelevant questions.

"Oh for God's sake shut up," he said to him at length, "it'll all be in the report."

He ascended the steps and let himself out through the kitchen door to inspect the rear of the house. He made notes about the sewage outlets from the bathrooms. He then traced the outfall from the sewerage systems, and followed the piping down towards a large cesspit near the river. This was most interesting, as it went absolutely nowhere near the mudslide at all. In fact it was on the opposite side of the house.

Once on the cesspit, he instructed the policeman to raise the lid, which he did with much grunting and heaving, but it all seemed to be in working order and smelt appropriately rich. It might need emptying in a couple of years, but apart from that everything appeared to be in good order.

He next decided to have a good look at the site of the mudslide itself. So he went around the outside of the house and approached from the lower side of the lawn. He made an assessment in his mind of the quantity of water that would have been needed to produce that kind of spillage. He guessed that the spill had covered an area in excess of two hundred square yards, and the volume of water would have to have been something like a hundred thousand gallons. It was just an initial guess, but there was absolutely no way that they were going to get anything like that amount of water out of the sewerage systems. After all, it was all fed by a tank in the attic, and any tank which could contain a hundred thousand gallons would have fallen through the building and into the cellar decades ago. Therefore, there had to be another source. He considered the possibility of a rain water collection system, but the house was connected to mains water.

He walked up the hill around the mud spill, and made brief notes about the area covered, the positioning of the wall, and the rough dimensions of the original pond. He could see what remained of this pond, partially hidden as it was by slumped vehicles. So if the water didn't come from the sewerage system it had to come from somewhere. He stood looking down on the scene of utter devastation and then he had it. It was very simple really; damn stupid that he hadn't seen it in the first place, after all the place was called Mill House for God's sake.

"Right, where's the bloody source," he said to himself and headed towards the rhododendron border.

Almost immediately he found himself in a slight dip in the lawn. 'Got it,' he said to himself. Then he walked as far as he could towards the rhododendrons, stopped and reverse tracked. There was no damn way he was going to try and fight his way through in the suit. So he made his way back past the security guard, who he ignored (even though the man did grunt something at him), out into the lane and turned right down to a gate. He opened the gate and made his way down towards where he assumed the leat would be. At first it looked like a hedge, but when he got closer he discovered that it concealed a deep millrace, and as expected it was full.

The policeman caught up with him and he pointed it out to him.

"That's the source of the problem," he said, and then marched off towards the river, before the young constable could ask any further questions. When he reached the far end, about three hundred yards across the field, he found what remained of a wall, still visible above water level.

It appeared to have been badly damaged at some point, allowing the water into the leat. He turned round and looked down the leat. It was overgrown with bramble, elder, hazel and oak saplings, and therefore must have been dry until fairly recently. The question then arose as to how the water had got into the leat, and how the wall had been damaged.

He called the young policeman over, "That's it," and pointed at the wall. The young policeman peered at it somewhat mystified while the surveyor made his way back to the house and his car.

Hurrying in his wake, the young policeman had thoughts, which the guard at the gate would have entirely sympathized with.

He had made sufficient notes to be able to charge his full fee. That would certainly do for now, and the Police could work out for themselves how the wall had been damaged. Most likely the winter floods he supposed, but he wasn't going to put that in print.

And he made his way back in the Jag to his club in Exeter. Once here, with a glass of brandy in his hand, he phoned the report to his secretary. She made notes in shorthand and then collected the references to the plans of the house and the maps of the area. Later she typed up her notes and added the stock sections he always insisted on. This made the report much longer, and he said more comprehensive. But she guessed it allowed him to charge more.

The following morning he checked it, changed a few words and by lunchtime it was on its way to the chief constable in Bidstable.

Chapter 16

A week after the mudslide, the three friends got together in the pub. They sat as usual staring sadly into their ciders.

The smoke from Archie's pipe hung pleasantly in the air above them.

"I can get half a pint to last a whole evening these days," said Archie almost to himself.

The other two grunted their agreement.

"Yes so what are we going to do next then, got any ideas?" asked Charlie.

Archie shook his head.

"No not so far, I think we've done our best. I can't think of anything else right now."

The three men had met on the day following the slide, and had agreed that they should avoid discussing their part in the incident, as Archie had said, "walls have ears!"

The following night Ivan had a nightmare. He dreamt he was back in Trinity again, and was trying to get up the ladder with his Bren gun. There were the thunder claps of shells exploding, and bullets flew past close overhead. Someone else was trying to get up the ladder with a mortar, and they struggled for foothold. Then a grenade came sailing through the hatch above them, hit a rung and rolled down at their feet. He woke sharply in a cold sweat and felt a great sense of relief sweep over him. He lay awake for a long time, trying to remember when he'd last had that particular nightmare.

The next evening he told the other two, "I think I might have an idea."

This was at least cheery news to Charlie and Archie. They had begun to believe that they were stuck with the cider, and nothing they could do; would ever bring their beloved Ferrets back.

"What you got in mind?" asked Archie, lowering his voice and looking over his shoulder to check for snoopers.

"Well," Ivan whispered, "do you know what I did in the war?"

"I thought you were farming," Archie replied.

"I was," confirmed Ivan, "but what else?"

"You didn't do nout else," Archie said, "you were here all the time, you never left.

"That's right," said Ivan, "however, I did do some war work."

"It's been over twenty year," said Archie.

Ivan massaged the back of his head for a while; then whispered "Twenty eight actually, so I think there's been enough time, we should be alright but you two will have to be very careful what you say to anybody."

"Why?" asked Charlie, again under his breath.

"Because if you go and spill the beans," Ivan explained quietly, "I'll be making mail bags at Her Majesty's pleasure for the next twenty years!"

"Oh," said Charlie, not at all clear on what they were talking about.

"So what you got in mind?" Archie asked.

"Well," explained Ivan, "in late 41, a few of us in the village. There were three of us in Somleigh, and I suppose there must have been other men in other villages, were recruited to fight the Nazis if they had invaded."

"I know bout that," said Archie, "I was in the Home Guard as well if you remember."

"No," said Ivan, "that's not what I mean at all."

"So what do you mean?" asked Archie.

"Well," he explained delicately again, "a small group of us were trained in sabotage techniques in addition to our work in the Home Guard, and we were rather well equipped."

"Saboteurs?" asked Archie, "I didn't know about that!"

"We had mortars, gas grenades, hand grenades, rifles; a whole arsenal in fact."

"We just had rifles, small arms and grenades," said Archie.

"And it's still all there," said Ivan slowly.

"What you are talking about?" asked Charlie.

"It was very very hush hush," explained Ivan, "they were supposed to collect it at the end of the war, but never did. And it's all still there."

"Where?" asked Charlie.

"Well that's the bit I can't tell you," explained Ivan, "but its all still there, I'm sure, although I've not looked since."

Archie was looking at Ivan intently.

"What about t'others?" he asked.

"Well," Ivan searched his memory. "One of them's dead, died of cancer about three years ago and the other one, well I don't know where he is, he disappeared years ago. I think he might have gone to Australia or something, but he's not around no more."

"So you are the only one that knows," said Charlie.

"I think so,"

"So what do you plan to do?" asked Archie, "if you've got all this stuff."

"Well I was just thinking about the gas grenades," said Ivan.

"Tear gas?"

"I was just thinking," explained Ivan, "if we let them off in their scullery or in that cave, that'll clear the place out and no mistaking."

Archie was non-committal, "sounds down right dangerous to me," he said, - "might work though."

'I'll have to give it some thought', Archie said to himself.

Charlie seemed game, "I would have thought that would do it."

"How long would it hang around in the house if we did let them off?" he asked, "Oh a few hours I suspect," said Ivan, "but it would certainly get them out. If they don't know where it's coming from, we can let them off at any time we like. That'll clear them out for sure."

Archie remembered tear gas; he'd been exposed to it at Aldershot once and hadn't liked it. Like washing your face in liquid pepper. He felt sure it would have a devastating impact - if there was enough.

"How many of them tear gas things have you got?" he asked.

"I dunno I haven't looked for almost thirty years," admitted Ivan.

"When we put them down there were crates and crates of the things."

"Why so many?" asked Charlie.

"Well the idea was that if you knew which way the wind was going and let off a whole load of them you could clear out a whole valley."

"Why?"

"If there were Nazis somewhere you didn't want them, you could clear them out with this stuff and then finish them off with trips or machine guns."

"Like booby traps or someit?" asked Archie

"That's it, just put them into a killing zone and take them out. It's quite easy to force them into a small area and then finish them off."

Charlie thought this was all rather unpleasant and preferred to think about Mill House.

"So, we let off a load of these grenades, they run out the house - what do they do next?"

"I don't know," said Ivan. "I suppose they'd call the police and try and find out what it was."

"And the police?" asked Charlie.

"Well I don't suppose they'd find anything," Ivan explained.

"They'd do a lot of digging to find out where it had come from, but they wouldn't be able to find anything in the way of residue, they'd assume it was something to do with the sewers again I suspect."

"Alright," Archie said at last "let's have a think about it for a day or two and see what goes on down there in the meantime."

The following day Ivan went for a walk in the woods. He spent some time standing behind a tree to see that he wasn't followed and took a few wrong turns just to throw any tracker off the scent. Once he was satisfied, he made his way to the bunker. For some strange reason, he couldn't quite remember, they'd called it Trinity. He found it much as it had been before, but heavily overgrown of course.

It took a lot of work to clear the brambles from the top, but eventually he found the lid. It had been cleverly designed to look like a mossy hummock. He stuck a crowbar under one edge and put weight on it. It snapped open with a crack; the cast iron had rusted into the frame. He pulled it out of the way and shone his torch down into the murky depths below.

The first thing he saw was his own reflection staring back up at him. It gave him a bit of a shock, as for a fleeting second he thought there was some one down there. And then the smell of cordite pulled him back through all those years, and he remembered the nights, and the dark and the silence.

They were brave young men. Tough and brave, and prepared to die for their country.

He could see the empty beer bottles they had abandoned, and wondered if the record player was still there. Beer and music had been recommended by top brass as an inflatable way of preventing brave young men crying for their mummies when the hatch was closed and the darkness closed in on them.

"Water," he said to himself as he looked down at his reflection. The site had been chosen fairly high up to try and avoid flooding, but with the span of time he assumed it had begun to fill up. He clambered down the ladder, taking care in case of loose rungs, but it was cast iron and seemed fairly solid. Pitch stood at top and looked down at him. He shone his torch cautiously at the water. Then stepped into it, and found it to be about six inches deep. Like a man stepping onto the moon, he was tempted to say, 'one small step', but refrained.

He pointed the torch towards the far end of Trinity and saw the boxes stacked where they had left them. He remembered that many of them contained food and bottled water. The plan had been that if the Nazis had invaded, they would have been stuck down here for months, coming out at night to run sabotage operations. In reality they suspected their life span was counted in days rather than months. But at that time they hadn't talked about such things.

All the boxes were all there, but some of the lower ones were saturated with water. He tried to ascertain which was which. The ones nearest the ground were green with mould and heavily water logged. He scratched a label on the lowest box.

"Oh bugger," he said to himself, "it's the bloody mortars!"

He guessed they had put them on the ground as they were much heavier than everything else. Even the cans of food weren't as heavy. "It's going to be quite a job," he said to himself, "I can't do it on my own."

There were thirty or forty cases in Trinity, and he had no idea which ones contained the tear gas. The mortars also worried him, the tubes were perfectly alright, but the mortars themselves might go off because of the water. He seriously considered doing something about it. They would need to be dried out at the very least. If this little lot went off, it could blow half the hillside away and kill anybody in the vicinity. He retraced his steps up the ladder and joined Pitch on the surface. After she had greeted him with much tail wagging, he put the hatch back into position and tried to rearrange the brambles as much as possible

- to conceal any evidence of his passing.

He made his way back to the Barton that night with thoughts bouncing round his head. If he was going to open it up and get stuff out, he was going to need a bit of help. But the Official Secrets Act was still a problem. This one would have to be played carefully.

Chapter 17

The following Tuesday Joanna took the afternoon off and went over to see Jim Lemon in South Moxton again. She had a few ideas that might help things along a little bit. She was aware that odd things were happening down at Mill House, and was vaguely suspicious that it had something to do with the three schemers in the bar. She had decided that whatever it was - if her suspicions proved correct - she wanted nothing what-so-ever to do with it. If as she suspected, they had gone beyond the law, she planned to keep to the right side of the law at all costs. Publicity after all, could be a problem.

She was escorted into Jim's Victorian office and sat staring at the dusty shelves and the tiny cluttered window above her. It took some time for him to appear and as she waited she took note of some of the names on his files. He obviously had most of the accounts books, as well as a few customer files. And from what she could see they seemed to go back to the 1880s. There was also a great collection of brew books which also seemed to stretch back even further. She guessed that it would take years to find the correct Ferrets formula in amongst that little pile. Eventually Jim appeared looking flustered and more like a cross between a lemon and a frog than ever. He apologized for the delay and explained that he'd been asked to change the brew yet again.

"Why?" asked Joanna

"We were told to change it three times in the last two weeks; apparently they are having problems selling it in London."

"Well at least that's positive," she said, "Do you think he'll go back to the old formula?"

"No he's dead against that," explained Jim, "I keep suggesting it and he keeps saying filthy things about it. No chance I'm afraid."

"Oh," Joanna said, "I could do with a change back, my customers are only drinking about a quarter of what they use to, I'm losing money Jim and I'm sure a lot of the other pubs are as well."

"Well you're right on that score," Jim said, "we're hardly selling anything in Devon, but he doesn't seem to care about that. He's only interested in London, and says we are going to keep on changing the formula until we get it right!"

"Can't you swap them back to the old brew mix and not tell him?" she asked.

"No he comes up here at least twice a week to taste it."

"You heard he got bitten?" asked Joanna.

"Yes, he was away for a few days after that," Jim confirmed "but he's back as vile-tempered as ever now. Bloody nuisance, I wish the dog had got his throat."

"Did you hear about the mudslide?"

"No, what's that?"

"Their sewers exploded right in the middle of a party about a week ago," explained Joanna.

"What, at Mill House?"

"Yes,"

"What caused that?"

"They don't know."

"Oh," he said.

"Jim," she asked, "what will he do if you get the mix right and the London sales increase?"

Jim massaged the back of his neck for a while and mulled it over, "I don't know, I hadn't thought about it."

"Say he wants to increase production. What's your maximum at the moment?"

"Well we can put out about twenty barrels a week at a stretch."

"And if he asked for fifty?"

"No, that's too much."

"So if you were selling fifty barrels a week and you couldn't supply what would he do?"

"I suppose he'd have to move production somewhere else," Jim acknowledged.

"And where might he take it if the market's in London?"

"Oh," said Jim, "I see what you mean; he'd take it up London way I suppose."

"And would you go with him?"

"Absolutely not, I'm not going to that bloody place. Anyway I expect he'd take the brew book and subcontract it to a London brewery."

"So," Joanna said quietly, "if you don't do what he wants he fires you and your staff. And if you do what he wants and he succeeds - he still fires you all. So what are you going to do Jim?"

"I hadn't rightly thought of it like that. It puts a different complexion on it."

"That's right Jim," she said.

"However" she continued after a short pause, "I have a couple of suggestions for you."

"Go on," he said slowly,

"Well," she said, "if he never gets the mix right, then he'll have to give up in the end won't he?"

"I suppose he might do, but he's a bloody minded sod."

"So," said Joanna "if he never got the brew right - then he wouldn't fire you would he?"

"I suppose not," Jim confirmed, "but he'd lose patience eventually."

"So what would he do then?"

Jim thought for a minute.

"Well he could either swap back to the original formula or he could sell the brewery."

"That's right," Joanna acknowledged.

"But he seems to know what he is doing, although I don't think much of his taste," Jim said.

"He's being fairly careful about modifying the brew mix and he will get it in the end, or he'll get something anyway."

"So Jim," said Joanna, "what if something were to accidentally fall into the mix and make all the brews that he tries distasteful?"

"I dunno - wouldn't he spot it?"

"Depends what it was that fell in by mistake wouldn't it," said Joanna.

"No, I couldn't do that - that would be wrong!"

"Yes that's right it would be," said Joanna, "but so would firing all your staff."

Jim stared at her in silence for a few moments and gulped silently to himself. What was he to do, he wasn't at all sure.

"Alright," said Joanna, "now, that's one option, but there is another one."

Jim was greatly relieved to hear it,

"Go on," he said.

"If," Joanna postulated, "if Customs and Excise did an inspection, would all your books be in order?"

"I think so, I've done my best to keep them up to date, I might be a bit antiquated in the methods I use but I'm sure it's all there."

"What about Richard Fox and his purchase of the brewery?" she asked.

"Well I got a bit on that I suppose."

"And what about the current VAT returns?" she asked.

"Well I haven't done them for a few months," he acknowledged.

"Why?"

"When Foxtradic bought the brewery, they started doing the VAT returns. I just do the bookkeeping; they do the VAT and corporation tax stuff now."

"So you've handed that over to them?" she asked.

"Well, not quite all of it, I still keep records of what we buy and sell. I couldn't do the books without it," he said.

"Ok," she prompted, "if they were buying other things, would you know about it?"

"Well no, I don't suppose I would. Not if they're doing the returns. No, I wouldn't see any of that," he gulped.

Joanna continued, "So is there anything that you might know - which Richard Fox would not like Customs and Excise to know about?" she asked.

"I not sure," he said, "I'll have to have a think about that!"

"You do that," she suggested.

"What would happen," she asked, "if he got a hefty demand for VAT or income tax?"

"What do you mean?" he gulped again, "like a really big one?"

"Yes," she said, "thousands, or tens of thousands."

"Ooh," he mulled to himself, "I suppose he'd have to come up with some cash pretty quick."

"That's right; otherwise they'd seize his assets wouldn't they?"

"Yes," he was following her now.

"So they might seize the brewery or he might have to sell it?"

"Yes," said Jim.

"Ok, in which case you'd be home and dry again. Someone else would take Ferrets over, and you could revert to the old brew."

"Yes," he said more cheerfully, "but I'd have to be a bit careful."

"Why?" asked Joanna.

"Well we work for Foxtradic don't we? So we can't go and give all their secrets away."

"But Jim," she said, "if you're requested to provide information by the Customs and Excise, it's the law; you have to give that information up. You can't start hiding it, because then it would be tantamount to fraud and you could go to prison."

"I suppose so," he said.

"You think about it," she said.

"Will do," he agreed.

She got up to leave. "Thanks for your time Jim, oh and by the way," she added slowly, "this conversation never took place, alright?"

His eyes sparkled, "what conversation?"

And she made her way back down the steps.

Jim sat behind his desk and thought about their conversation. But mostly he thought about Joanna. 'It wasn't often you get brains and beauty in one package' was his first thought. His second thought was to wish he was a bit younger. His third was that he wished he was a lot younger.

Then he wondered why he hadn't married a woman like Joanna, she would have been great for the brewery. Instead he'd married a respectable local girl, who had him sleeping on the sofa, eating broccoli (which he hated) three times a week, demanded no shoes in the house, snored like a water buffalo and had him on an eternal diet.

Fortunately the brewery was just around the corner from the bakers which had an excellent selection of cakes, and Mole Valley Farmers up the road had a good stock as well.

Probably Joanna as a wife would have run the brewery a lot better than he had, and maybe it would be him in an apron vacuuming the lounge. But thinking of such things was like crying over spilt milk.

The next morning before he left for work, Jim took a five pound bag of a white powder from his scullery and put it in his car. A few spoonfulls of that would turn the mix alright he thought.

Chapter 18

When the report arrived on his desk in Bidstable Police headquarters Inspector Carpenter was in one of his moods again.

"Why the hell are you bringing this to me?" he asked.

The Sergeant on duty said, "It came in addressed to you Sir."

"I know that," the Inspector complained.

"It's marked for your attention Sir,"

"I know it's marked for my bloody attention, but what the hell are you bringing it to me for?" he asked.

"Because that's what it says," said the Sergeant - beginning to be annoyed.

The inspector stared at the document.

"So what's my section?" he asked, assuming the sergeant was just a little bit on the thick side.

"Crime Sir."

"Yes, so why are you bringing me sewerage problems in Somleigh?" he asked.

The Sergeant was obviously two pennies short of the full shilling, and should have been fired years ago he thought.

"Well Sir, it's err, yes, it's a sewerage problem," confirmed the Sergeant, "but there's something in the back and in the summary about potential crime."

"Oh for God's sake!" said the inspector. "Alright, alright you can go," and the sergeant stamped out, slamming the door behind him.

Inspector Carpenter was not a man to suffer fools gladly and the Sergeant had been sorely trying his patience.

"Alright," he said to himself. 'If I've got to look at the bloody thing," and he pulled it across the desk and started reading. "Ok, ok, yeh ok, lots of people injured yeh I know about that, but it's not my section," he grumbled to himself. 'Alright, alright, OK, surveyors report,' he turned the pages over and flicked through the summary. 'It's that bloody pompous Lord whatsit again, where he could do with one page he likes to put thirty in.

"Ok," he went through the various sections, there were sixteen pages on the sewerage system alone, and that wasn't the problem, well didn't seem to be. Eventually he found the paragraph that the Sergeant had been alluding to.

"Yeh," it said that somebody might have deliberately damaged the wall, let the water in and had caused the problem. "Oh for God's sake," he grumbled to himself. "Things are going on like this all the time in this God forsaken county. Fences fall down, trees collapse on houses and cars, roofs are damaged by wind, can you expect walls to last for bloody ever?'

"Oh Hell," he said to himself at last, and buzzed back to the sergeant.

"Sergeant, I've got a job for you."

"Yes Sir," said the sergeant reappearing.

"Alright," said the Inspector, "you brought me the report, so you can go and have a look at this dam wall."

"Yes Sir," said the sergeant.

"Find out if it was smashed on purpose, a bit of standard country vandalism, or if it just fell down."

"Yes Sir," said the sergeant and disappeared.

"That would fix the bugger, every time he tried to dump something on him, he would give it back to him and send him away to sort it out. He was good at delegation and it was the best tactic he'd got."

Then he went back to his real work, planning the next golf tournament.

The sergeant however, far from being annoyed, went back to his desk, phoned a certain young lady in Somleigh, and asked her what was for dinner. She had a nice bit of minced beef and some fresh new potatoes and did he fancy a fresh bit of rough?

"I'll be with you in a couple of hours. I've just got something to do outside the village, and then I'll be straight up."

"Naughty boy!" she said.

Then he phoned his wife and said he'd be late, very late, as the Inspector had sent him on a Police job.

Then he went down to the car park, took a pool squad car and headed for Somleigh. He loved working for the Police, and Inspector Carpenter was one of his favorites. Although he was pompous and full of bluster, he was incredibly easy to manipulate.

He'd been with them for twenty-one years and he knew the system better than anybody else in the station. Generally they got their Inspectors from London, where they'd failed with the Met. And they ended up being relegated down to Devon. He supposed it was like being put on traffic duty. They generally retired after a year or two, and then they would send them another head-case to replace the last.

It took him about an hour to get to Somleigh and another few minutes to reach the house. He didn't need to go up to the house, so he parked in the lane. He took the report out, extracted the plans and headed down towards the river.

When he got there he had a good look at the wall. Yes it certainly looked like somebody had given it a hell of a thump with something. He could see tractor tracks in the field, so somebody had been working there recently.

He'd have to go and ask the farmer if he'd done it by mistake. He'd deny it of course, but it would be another excuse to go and see Helen. So he made a quick sketch of the area in his notepad, made a few notes about the destruction of the wall and then hopped back into the squad car and headed into the village. She was doing cottage pie, and he particularly liked cottage pie. He wondered what was for afters.

Chapter 19

On a warm June evening the group gathered in the drawing room. They slouched around the Georgian fireplace in armchairs and sofas, with their chemist Bob chairing the meeting as normal.

Most of the injuries had now healed, and only the bandage on Mick's wrist evidenced the events of just a few weeks before. They had decided that they had no enthusiasm for any further parties that year. What with the repairs, and their state of depression, they had no intention of inviting a single visitor if at all possible. There was some doubt as to whether any would agree to come even if they were invited.

Anyway, they needed to do some more work on the album, as the record company was exerting some pressure.

Bob began by discussing at some length the chemicals he planned to use, a strange mixture of LSD, caffeine and for some strange reason Paracetamol. "Reduces the symptoms of discomfort," he explained.

The plan was they would have a light supper and begin the next experiment at eleven o'clock at night. They were specifically told to avoid alcohol during the trial, and for eight hours beforehand. Sometimes he let them drink, sometimes he forbade it. It seemed to depend on all the chemicals inscribed in his little book.

"Today," he said, "I'm trying this mixture as it is more effective without the alcohol than with it." he explained. "I've noticed that when we add alcohol, it tends to end in a fight. I've added a very small amount of the toad exudate, and if it goes well, we can try increasing the concentration."

So they ate a light supper, and then took their instruments and trooped through to the studio next to the kitchens.

The glass house had cost a lot of money, it was made of welded steel, and the glass was bulletproof. It had been designed to prevent them getting out and hurting themselves. Additionally if there were problems inside, the security guards could fetch them out and straightjacket them.

But with over two feet of mud in it, it was out of action for the time being, cleaning would take another few weeks. So they had been forced to use the second studio instead. Bob locked them in and they began by playing some warming up tracks before starting.

Once they felt in the mood, they went to the hatch, and the vials and glasses of water were pushed through from the kitchen.

"Ok, go ahead," said Bob, and the four men poured the powder into their glasses and drank it down quickly. They then resumed their seats and continued to play as before. It was a long session, because the drugs didn't seem to kick in for at least an hour. However they eventually started to feel euphoric and the music began to flow.

Bob, sitting in the kitchen was pleased. The recording equipment was picking up

some neat stuff. Whenever he felt the music was worthy of note, he would
make a note of the time. They would of course listen to the whole track over the
next few days, but any hints were useful. They had found this more effective
than trying transcribing the music as they went.

Suddenly Shaun started doing some really very strange screaming and shouting.
For an instant they thought a straightjacket would be required. However, he
seemed to be quite content playing his guitar and yelling and screaming at the
same time. Some of the noises he made were close to musical and reminded
Bob more of Japanese rhythms than anything else. They would be fascinated
listening to that tomorrow he thought.

Nothing particularly unusual took place that evening, and the party broke up at
about two. He gave each man a light sleeping draught and they were lead up the
stairs to their beds. For security they were chained to their beds with a padded
cuff round one ankle. Bob had explained that because of the novel formulae he
was using, he'd no idea whether there might be lag effects. These could induce
further disturbances many hours after imbibing the dose.

After Bob had explained what 'imbibing' meant, they'd agreed to this, not
knowing whether it was true or not but feeling it was better to be chained, than
to risk throwing themselves out of the nearest window. They had heard about
things like that with LSD users.

Chapter 20

When Mickel woke up he immediately knew that something wasn't quite right.
Apart from anything else, he could see the sky. That in itself was unusual. What
appeared to be even more unusual was where he was. He found he was lying
prone on what appeared at first glance to be a tangled mass of sticks and twigs
spread out around him in a bowl shape. He sat up to try and get his bearings,
and crawled up to the edge of the bowl. Peered over, he was astonished to find
that he was at the top of a tree, in the middle of a great forest. He wondered
how in God's name he'd got up there. All this was very unusual, but what shook
him more than anything else, was the fact that the sky appeared to be full of
huge birds. He speculated briefly on where the hell he was. However looking up
again he noticed one of the vulture like creatures gliding slowly down towards
him. It hovered above him and let out a terrific screech. He guessed its
wingspan must be something over forty feet. Suddenly he understood where he
was. He was in the bloody thing's nest.

Panic overtook him, and he headed for the edge to try and get out as quickly as
possible. He found to his intense surprise that he seemed to be restrained in
some way. Looking down at his ankle, he discovered to his horror that a snake
had wrapped itself around one foot. He pulled fiercely and after a few
tremendous heaves the snake relinquished its hold on the sticks. As the sticks

came loose, he was appalled to see many more snakes within the body of the nest and he resolved to remove himself from the vicinity as rapidly as possible. He took a flying leap out of the nest, landing on a branch some feet below. It knocked the wind out of him, but after some seconds of heavy breathing he recovered sufficiently to plan his route down the tree. He was at least a hundred feet from the ground, but peering down; he discovered that there were some liana like vines, which hung from the upper branches to the ground. He crawled across, grabbed one, and began sliding down it. He lost some skin on his hands and feet but eventually reached the ground, if not un-blooded at least in one piece.

He wondered what the hell he was to do next; the sky was still full of the god-awful birds. Around him the great forest spread out in all directions. Then, as no other sensible option presented itself, he turned and ran. After some minutes he found himself in a clearing, and crossed rapidly to the far side. Loud squawks were still coming from the sky above him, but at least the canopy gave him cover. Odd rustlings came from the undergrowth, and although he could not see any other wildlife, he regarded all such noises with great suspicion.

After some minutes, he became aware that he was being followed. Something appeared to be stalking him. Whatever it was he couldn't see it. When he stopped to listen, it stopped. He decided that the place of greatest safety would be in the trees again, and searched around for one with easy handholds. He found one, and sheered up it as fast as he could. Underneath him the grass parted and something large and black appeared out of the undergrowth. It looked up at him and growled in a most threatening manner, displaying a fine set of canines as long as boar tusks.

He had no idea what the creature was, but as it seemed to be well equipped with both claws and teeth. Reason; which hinted that the creature knew little about British fair play, and was not well acquainted with the powers of the police, compelled him to climb higher. Below him the creature lay siege to the tree, and then started making explosive leaps to try and reach him. The higher he climbed, the more infuriated it seemed to become. What remained of his pajamas were torn to shreds and his already battered and bruised arms and feet were even more torn than they had been when he'd made the descent from the nest. When he eventually reached the highest bough, he discovered that something had got there before him.

Sitting on a small bough was a medium sized animal, which reminded him more of a sort of porcupine than anything else. It regarded him with great ferocity, and as he backed himself against the main trunk, it moved towards him with some purpose. When it reached his feet he came to the conclusion that it was even less informed about the law than the furious creature below, so he let out a yell and jumped.

He bounced painfully from branch to branch, and as he neared the ground the pain became even more intense. He alighted finally with some force on a large bough about thirty feet from the ground. At last his strength gave out and he fainted.

Back at the house similar horrors had marred the sleep of the other musicians. The unfortunately after effects of several hundred times too much toad extract had had fairly virulent effects on each the four men. Mickel in his tree had had the misfortune of coming face to face with the only resident leopard in the whole parish of Somleigh.

This was the first time the unassuming and secretive cat had been treed by a naked human but had responded in the appropriate fashion. It had arched its back, and growled furiously, and put out all claws in a fairly effective show of threat. The naked human had let out an ear shattering scream and leapt from the branch. The leopard, convinced more than ever that all humans were bad news, had descended the tree and disappeared rapidly into the night.

Shaun, who had thought he was in a cave deep underground populated by giant ants, had screamed his head off, escaped from the house, and run pajama clad into the river.

The other two members had not faired any better. One had thrown himself headlong out of the window irrespective of glass or wood, and had landed in a mangled heap on the lawn below. He had only been saved by the pile of lawn clippings that Charlie had deposited there the day before.

The last man had been fully restrained by the shackle around his ankle but had dragged the bed around the room three or four times before collapsing from exhaustion.

Bob, Richard Fox and the minders had been woken by seriously worrying noises, and had at first thought the dogs were back. But they had quickly discovered that members of the group were on the loose. The debate was then whether or not to call the police. They decided caution was the better option.

The one member of the group who was still in his room and still attached to the bed could not be approached and was like a wild animal.

All they could do was to try and protect him from himself. And they did try very hard, unsuccessfully as it turned out, to get him into a straightjacket. In the end they realized that they had no option, but to call the police whether they liked it or not. Shortly after that they found an unconscious body on the lawn, and an ambulance was called.

The Police arrived directly, and soon requested an explanation for the night's events.

Bob, worried by the drugs issue, said they had been drinking too much.

Fortunately the Police accepted this without too much preamble, and got down to the matter in hand.

At first light, Police search parties were sent out. Bob and Richard were secretly very worried that that they might lose at least one member of the group, possibly permanently. The drummer, who had thrown himself out of his window, was in a very bad way indeed, and had broken several ribs, an arm and a leg. He was taken away shortly after five by an ambulance crew who also suspected internal injuries. The man who had pulled the bed around his room was ambulanced off shortly after. It was regarded as something of an achievement, as the bed was solid oak and must have weighed nearly half a ton. With him, it was more a case of muscle damage than broken bones, but he would certainly be very sore when he woke up.

Shaun was discovered a little while later, when he pulled himself bedraggled, wet and extremely cold from the river. The after effects of the drug seemed to wear off after a few hours and he was perfectly coherent by the time he reappeared in the house. When questioned, he gave a rather hazy picture of the night's events. He knew something untoward had happened, and could remember parts of it, but couldn't actually remember with any great lucidity how it had all started. Something about ants they could understand, but the rest of it seemed to be hazy even to him.

"Perhaps like a nightmare," Bob commented to Fox, "it wears off after you've woken up, and a couple of hours later you can't remember the thing at all."

"Keep it down, we don't want the Police hearing too much," responded Fox.

Finally Mickel was the only remaining member of the group unaccounted for. At eleven thirty that morning, a call came in to the Police from a local market gardener, who had discovered what remained of a man under an oak tree at the bottom of his garden.

"I think he's dead," he said, "I prodded him with my rake, but can't get any movement out of him."

He was asked if he'd checked his pulse.

"No didn't want to get too close, he's such a mess, blood all over the shop," he said.

When the ambulance finally arrived they discovered the corpse was actually still breathing, and so he was trucked off to Bidstable hospital to join the other three.

Later that day Bob spent many hours, although completely relieved that they were all alive, trying to understand what had gone wrong. He couldn't work it out at all, although there had been a tiny amount of toad exudate in the doses he'd prepared the previous evening, it was so small, it couldn't possibly have accounted for the chaos which had ensued. Additionally, it hadn't happened until they were all asleep in the middle of the night, well after the experiment had ended. There had to be an answer, he would have to reanalyse the formula. He had a little left over, so he set to work to double check what had actually been in the dose that they had taken the previous evening.

He had a feeling he wasn't going to like the results.

Chapter 21

A few days later, Archie and Charlie joined Ivan at Greenly Barton. It had been prearranged Ivan would blindfold them before taking them up to Trinity. Initially they had objected strongly to this. In the end Ivan had bribed them with Hockings ice cream, and explained his difficult position, and in the end his terms were agreed to.

They would help him move boxes, but the location of Trinity was to be kept from them. They drank whisky in the kitchen, before heading out in Ivan's van. Pitch was left in her kennel as Ivan didn't want her getting loose again. Dogs and explosives didn't seem a very good combination. He had a vision of her retrieving a smoking explosive and blowing the lot of them to kingdom come. He blindfolded the two passengers, and then drove quite a confusing, circuitous and zigzagging route, to prevent them locating the place again, even if they tried. He was conscious that Archie knew the area better than the back of his hand, and unless completely confused he would have a fair chance of finding it again. So after getting himself lost a couple of times, going down overgrown lanes he'd never even noticed before, he made his way to Trinity, driving up the chase through the woods to reach it.

Eventually he got them out, removed their blindfolds and led them up to Trinity. He showed them the entrance and the three men removed the lid, and peered down into the dark interior.

"I'll go down first," explained Ivan, "and guide you down."

They nodded their agreement, and he climbed down with a torch between his teeth. He then shone it up at them as they descended the ladder. Once all three were inside, he noticed the water had dropped slightly since his last visit. They shone their torches at the stacked boxes at the far end.

"So which is which?" asked Archie.

Ivan scratched his head, "Well I don't really know anymore, it's been so long, I'm sure we made notes, but I just can't remember."

They went across to the boxes and scraped the mould from some of the labels. It was soon clear that there was some sort of system involved. The layers alternated between food and water, and munitions.

It sparked Ivan's memory, "Yes, I think I can remember, the idea was that if we were attacked we could get to the munitions quickly, so at least we had something we could get our hands on, even if we had to throw the odd box of food on the floor."

They rigged up an A frame using three poles and some binder twine, and hung a pulley from it. Then with Charlie pulling on the rope they placed the boxes they needed one at a time into a rope sling. Charlie then hoisted them to the surface and piled them to one side. They took out about six boxes initially; mostly smoke grenades and tear gas. There were one or two others that they couldn't identify, so Ivan suggested they hoist them up anyway, as they might be of some use. Finally, when they cleared the food cases, they got down to the mortars. Archie wasn't particularly keen on picking them up, as they were so wet.

But Ivan said, "We've got no choice, in these damp conditions they could go off at any time."
Archie agreed eventually, muttered a quick prayer and a few expletives, and they slid the sodden boxes across the floor and placed them dripping in the sling.
Then Ivan went up top, to help with the hoisting. They carried the boxes to the van, and loaded until its springs creaked. Then re-blindfolded, with Charlie and Archie squeezed into the passenger seat, Ivan drove them round another confusing and complicated route to Three Bridges.
They opened the gate and drove up to the quarry. Then they carried them one at a time into the cavern, piled them in the widest part, and threw an old blanket over them.

Chapter 22

When the hospital reports arrived on Inspector Carpenter's desk, he was furious.
"What the hell are these doing on my bloody desk," he shouted at the Sergeant.
"The Chief Constable thought they should come to you Sir," said the Sergeant.
"Why?" asked the Inspector.
"He says that it might be linked to the previous events at Mill House."
"Oh God, I suppose you suggested that," said the Inspector.
"No Sir, it was his idea," said the Sergeant.
"Alright, get out," said the Inspector.
The Sergeant went back to the duty desk, contemplating many happy evenings with a certain friend in Somleigh.
Meanwhile the Inspector decided that he'd better look at the hospital reports after all.
He stared at the damned things with a jaded eye.
"Yes – yes - yes he'd heard of Cordaxe, and yes - he'd come across them in the past.
He'd seen them in the papers while he was in the Met. They were supposed to be the 'drug band' or some such, and it was fairly obvious what had happened - they'd taken an overdose of something or other, and had behaved like complete bloody idiots.
From the reports they were extremely lucky that none of them were killed.
Three legs broken, two arms, and lots of contusions, fractures and so on.
"Serve them bloody right," was his opinion, "but 'what's it got to do with me?" followed on closely, as well as more seriously, "how do I off load it onto someone else?"
He read on through the documents, yes, it was fairly obvious that it shouldn't be his section. "C.R.I.M.E." he'd had to spell it out to the Sergeant, and the Sergeant had said, "Yes Sir, but the Chief Constable said….."

Actually he didn't believe this at all, but the one thing he'd learnt in the Met was not to disturb your Chief unless your life depended on it, and then only in direst of circumstances.

After staring at the thing for half an hour, he eventually bundled it up and took it down to narcotics.

"Joe this is one of yours,"

Joe looked up at him blankly.

"Mill House I suppose,"

"Yes, how did you know?"

"I had a word with the Chief, that's your baby!"

"Oh come on Joe, this is ridiculous - I'm crime - you're narcotics!"

Joe didn't agree.

"No chance," he said, "Look at the hospital report and see what they took."

Inspector Carpenter leafed briefly through the document, "LSD suspected," he read.

"Serves them bloody well right," he added.

Joe said, "You're going to have to go and talk to them and find out what they're up to."

"I doubt if they know themselves. Anyway, I know sod all about narcotics."

"You're prevaricating again," said Joe, "you worked in the drug squad in the Met, so that doesn't wash. Just go and find out what you can, if you think they're dealing let me know and I'll have a look at it."

And that was the end of that.

Inspector Carpenter was not a happy man that afternoon, his ulcer was giving him trouble again. He considered walking into the town and getting something from a chemist. In the end his temper was assuaged by instructing the Sergeant and a couple of constables to go and take statements from the other people in the house.

The Sergeant at first delighted, rapidly descended into gloom when he was told to take the Constables with him. He swore furiously under his breath, and wondered if the Inspector had got wind of his assignations in Somleigh.

Chapter 23

Joanna drove to Taunton on a pleasantly warm Wednesday evening in late June. It had been a lovely day and she'd had a walk round Somleigh earlier in the day and was in a thoroughly good mood.

The birds were nesting, there were squirrels in the trees, everything was right with the world and it was heaven to be living in such a beautiful part of the country. When she reached Taunton she was feeling thoroughly euphoric.

She parked the car, went up to the flat and checked the appointment book. She had three that evening, a Surveyor who came all the way from Bodmin, an

Accountant from Yeovil and her friend the VAT man from Bristol. She cleaned the place up a little, and then put the Hoover away and donned her costume. "I must have put on a little weight," she said to herself, "it doesn't usually stretch quite this tight." She arranged the bottles on the drinks trolley and poured a gin and tonic for her first guest.

Normally he didn't get a drink until he behaved himself, but he'd been good last time. The costume was definitely pinching this week. It made her think more about whether she wanted to continue doing it or not. Yes, it had been a great way of earning a bit of extra cash in the early days, but she didn't need it any more.

The rental income from fifteen properties in Somleigh was far more than she could get teaching public schoolboys how to behave!

But the risk was always there. While she'd been building the businesses, there had been much less risk of being recognised, no one could possibly associate her with the village. But now that she was reasonably well to do, and gradually becoming better known, the risk had increased, and she was beginning to feel that it was close to being unacceptable.

She would miss it of course; after all she enjoyed it just as much as they did. And what would her clients do if she told them she was going to retire?

Well... she contemplated this bleak prospect. Some of them might respond very badly indeed. She suspected one or two would try and find her again. They'd built up what was to all intents and purposes - an addiction. She wondered about this, but could see no clear way through, unless of course she were to die! "That might be a possible exit," she thought to herself, "if Joanna de Fleece were to have an unfortunate accident with a heavy lorry...."

'Then they wouldn't come looking for her would they?'

As she sat and waited for her first client, she began to plan her demise.

Eventually he turned up, reasonably on time and received the customary treatment. The second was a couple of minutes late but behaved himself by and large. He had failed to attend on a previous occasion some months before, so she gave him a particularly good belting. He wouldn't be able to sit down for a day or two; she hoped the discomfort would remind him not to miss their appointments in future.

Eventually the Customs and Excise chap arrived, red faced and out of breath. But he was grinning and was pleased himself.

He took his coat off and presented her with a manila folder.

"Here you are," he said, puffing, "It's a full report,"

She had a brief glance through the contents while he removed his clothing.

There was quite a bit on Mr Fox and Foxtradic. It seemed quite comprehensive, and would take some time to go through.

She was pleased with him, very pleased. She agreed to give him a couple of free sessions. He was delighted about that. Actually - a hundred pounds per session was a lot of money for him and the deception game that he played with his wife, about the cost of the boat and the Calais regatta were difficult to substantiate. Yes, there was a boat, and there was even a Calais regatta, but the costs weren't anywhere near as much as he claimed. If she ever happened to quiz anyone in the Yacht club as to how much it all cost, she would immediately spot his 'cooking of the books'.

He left shortly before ten. She took the precious envelope and headed back to Somleigh. It had been a most entertaining day. But Cassandra de Gate must meet her end!

She also she had a wonderful collection of documents on Mr Richard Fox. She was still contemplating what she was going to do with the portfolio, when she reached the pub and let herself in through the back door.

Chapter 24

When finally the group was reunited at Mill House, they met to express their fury to Bob. Not only had they suffered, oh-boy had they suffered, but they had also had to spend the last few days lying to nurses, doctors and the police.

"What the hell did you give us?" they asked.

He stammered his apologies.

"Something went wrong with the mix, there was a lot more of the – err - toad extract in there than I had planned."

"How the bloody hell did that happen?" they asked.

"I'm not sure," he confessed.

"You don't know how we suffered," Mickel said.

Shaun exploded, "I've had enemas, I've had my stomach pumped, I was inside a steam tent for three days trying to warm up!"

Mickel interrupted, "you were lucky, you didn't have two broken bloody legs to contend with!"

He was now confined to a wheelchair.

"How the hell am I supposed to play music sitting in this damn thing?" he asked.

They had a private meeting shortly after, from which Bob was specifically excluded, and they discussed firing the man.

"We can't rely on him," Shaun said. "If he starts filling us up with that kind of shit, we'll all end up dead!"

A very disgruntled group sat down to dinner that evening. Bob was in the doghouse and no mistake. He was sure it wasn't his fault, but he could find no other door to lay it at. He apologised repeatedly and declared that was absolutely sure it was nothing to do with him.

"Don't be bloody stupid, there is no one else to blame!"

He could see no way out of it.

In the end he said, "Look if you want me to resign I will."

But in the end they agreed to give him one more chance.

As it was, they didn't feel much like any further experiments for a while. Not only were they still in extremely poor health, broken bones, cuts, bruises and abrasions, but they also still had problems with their stomachs.

Meat - caused them real problems, vomiting during dinner could be most unsettling, particularly the unexpected projectile sort!

And the problems they were having at the other end were too unpleasant to discuss.

In the end, they decided that any further forays into the fascinating world of chemicals were completely out for the time being. In fact, most of them agreed they didn't even want to touch alcohol.

"I'll do fruit juice for the time being," said Shaun, after having hit a bust of Napoleon with vomit from twenty feet.

"Bob, you've tuned us all into T totallers!" added one of the others.

Over the following few days they spent their time going over the tapes that had been made of their previous recording sessions. They worked on improving on the recording, and began to develop the themes.

One afternoon, they sat in the drawing room, and listened to the tape they had made on the evening prior to their stay in Barnstaple Hospital. Two of the security guards were with them and were able to explain what was going on. There was great entertainment when Shaun started his screaming and strange vocalisations which were very interesting. Defiantly very different, and they wondered how they could use it in their act. They tried to get Shaun to reproduce it, but, not being a vocal performer - he was a guitarist after all - he objected strongly and when he did have a go, the results weren't worth writing home about.

"Perhaps we could get a singer," suggested Mickel.

Shaun agreed "Sure but it depends on what you're after, if you're after the kind of noise I was making on that tape, we'll need someone with a bit of flexibility."

Eventually it was left at that, possibly a tie-in with an opera singer. Mickel agreed to mention it to the record company.

Chapter 25

Back in the bar of The Royal Oak, debate raged as to the cause of the events at Mill House. The news had leaked out that they'd been in hospital, but exactly what had happened was still a mystery.

The man who had discovered Mickel in his garden had spoken about the event at some length, and had been getting free drinks on it for over a week.

"He was a real mess," he declared, "I thought he was dead at first, and I wanted to see if I could resuscitate him, but they told me not to touch him"

"When the ambulance came, they said he was still alive. I thought he was dead, he certainly looked like a corpse."

"But didn't you see he was breathing?" they asked.

"No, I had no idea, he looked that dead, and he was a real funny colour, like ash white."

Eventually they reached the conclusion that they'd taken something they shouldn't have.

"Can't expect anything better of people like that," said Archie.

The others nodded their agreement.

Ivan went to fetch more half pints of cider.

When he had returned, he sat and watched as Archie tried to light his pipe.

"There's a reasonable chance that they'll kill themselves, without us needing to help them along the way," Ivan whispered.

They thought about this for a while, but in the end they concluded that they weren't in a fit state to do anything very much.

"One of them's in a wheelchair," Charlie told them, "the others are walking around with their arms strapped up in funny positions - one of them was pulled out of the river."

One of the tame heavies had become friendly with Charlie, and had told him some of the gory details.

"Yes, one of them was in the river," he confirmed. "The other one was in someone's garden."

"We know about that," said Ivan, "what about the other two?"

"Oh, one of them landed on my lawn clippings, the other one never got out of the house, but damaged himself chucking furniture around."

"Furniture?"

"Drugs," explained Charlie, "they didn't know what they were doing."

"Well that's bloody obvious," said Ivan.

"So what's to do next?" Archie asked in a whisper.

The three men looked at each other with blank faces.

"Well," Ivan said. "We still have that third option don't we?"

The other two knew what he was talking about.

"So are we going to use it or not?"

There was silence for a while, while the three of them contemplated this prospect.

"We've got it all prepared," said Ivan. "All it needs is a match, no work at all."

Still silence.

"Perhaps we ought to wait until they're up and about," Archie said at length. "If they can't get out of their wheelchairs we'll kill the buggers."

"That's a point," admitted Ivan, "let's wait until they are all up and walking again, before we do anything."

They nodded to themselves.

It seemed like a good plan, although they wanted them out, they had no intention of killing them in the process. Twenty years making mailbags, as Ivan had said, didn't seem a particularly pleasant prospect.

Chapter 26

It took Joanna some weeks to go through the report. It was extremely comprehensive. There were copies of Customs and Excise documents, income tax returns, bank information and VAT returns. There were also copies of documents relating to the purchase of Ferrets Brewery - which must have come from the company's house. It was exactly what she needed, and it gave her a huge amount of information as to the machinations of Foxtradic and the man Fox himself.

For one thing, he'd bought the properties and a number of other businesses from Cordaxe for next to nothing.

If that wasn't fraud, she didn't know what was. Additionally somehow or other her friend had managed to get hold of Fox's income tax returns. The man was paying virtually no tax at all, and obviously lying outrageously about his income. What she really needed was someone with a good financial brain, who could go through it with a fine toothcomb. She needed some indication as to the length of his prison term, or what the fine would be if the authorities go their hands on the documents.

The one thing she didn't want to do, was spill the beans, at least not before she had made ample use of the documents. There were things she needed Mr Fox to do first.

In the end she went back to Nick Trout. He had a good knowledge of financial matters and readily agreed to help. They went through the documents together, after dinner at his house in Exeter. On one sheet of paper they scribbled down how much he was avoiding paying and on another sheet of paper they added up how many years in jail he would serve or what the fine might be if the facts came out.

After an evening of great amusement and much laughter, they decided that Richard Fox would serve something in the region of fifteen years if both the Customs and Excise and the Inland Revenue got their hands on the documents. The chances were that there would be a massive fine as well; in fact Nick said it would almost certainly bankrupt him.

"So what are you going to do with it?" he asked Joanna.

Joanna played with her necklace for a while.

"I'm not sure," she said, "I think I might offer him a chance to mend his ways."

"I don't think there's much chance of that, not in a million years!" said Nick looking at the folder in front of him, "the man's obviously a complete scoundrel!"

"Well… maybe I'll let him mend his ways a little bit, before he goes to prison.

"He'll just try all the harder to cover his tracks," said Nick.

"Oh yes," said Joanna, "but there's enough here to convict him, so that doesn't matter much, we've got plenty of evidence."

"That's true," said Nick.

"So what's your next move?"

"I haven't decided yet, but I've got some thoughts."

"Anyway, I never did ask you where you got all this."

"No you didn't did you!" she replied.

They laughed together over another drink, before she thanked him and headed back to Somleigh. She reached the pub in a rainstorm after eleven that night. Nick had been tremendously helpful and she very grateful for his advice.

The only issue outstanding was when she was going to meet with Richard Fox and…. how she was going to broach the subject of fifteen years in jail to him! He might after all get nasty and attack her. That was quite within the bounds of possibility. He might even try to knock her on the head, or cause her to have a nasty accident! With fifteen years in jail at stake, she could certainly see that he might.

Chapter 27

It wasn't until mid-July that it became evident to Charlie that the group were up and about again. He spotted them hobbling out to watch the building work. They'd extended the parking area and created a culvert. This should drain away any water that might flow from the Millrace in the future. The wall had been repaired, and the lower patio had been restored to its previous condition. There was little or no evidence to suggest that a catastrophe has so recently made such a mess of the house and garden.

They limped painfully around the building site, asking the builders inane questions. Peering through the doors into the Mill room, they saw that the glasshouse had been bucked and twisted by the force of the mud. It would have to be re-built. Considering what had happened to them, they seemed to be remarkably cheerful. Charlie supposed they were just relieved to be alive.

When the three men met in the bar that night, he told them the group were up and about.

"It's probably about time," he suggested, "that we did something with the gas grenades."

Ivan was relieved, "About bloody time too," he said, "that should get them out of the place once and for all. If they can't go in the house - what with the gas, they'll get in their dam cars and head straight head back to London."

The other two sincerely hoped he was right.

They chose a Thursday evening, mainly because nothing much happened in the house on a Thursday.

"It's all quiet on a Thursday and we won't hurt anybody else in the process,"

Ivan said.

"What time do we let them off?" Charlie asked.

"After they've gone to bed I should think, well fairly late anyway," Ivan suggested.

"What time do you suggest?"

The three men contemplated the hour of the night that would best suit their purposes. Eventually it was plumbed that eleven o'clock was probably quite a good time. So eleven o'clock on Thursday night it was to be. Little preparation was needed. All they had to do was to ensure the scullery door was slightly ajar and to move the cupboard an inch or two away from the wall. Then light the fuses and retire to a safe distance.

Chapter 28

Maureen in her sewing room had finally got the equipment working properly. She'd bought a larger more powerful battery, and had obtained a better aerial from the manufacturer.

This had meant that for the last few weeks the reception had been almost perfect. She very rarely missed any part of a conversation now and could hear almost everything that took place. The chatter in the bar was much easier to understand, and it was almost as if she was at the next table. She found that by changing the transmitter batteries frequently she could also get even better reception. That involved unpicking the stitching and sewing up again afterwards, but it was a small price to pay!

Events had unfolded in a most unusual manner. In fact she had been attending the hairdresser's slightly more frequently than of late. Her weekly visits now became quite an event for her, and she took great interest in the local gossip, particularly about the events at Mill House.

The mauling incident had bypassed her and she had understood little of went on at the time. Similarly she had heard about the mudslide, but all reports had been second hand. She was suspicious of course, but as she had no evidence, she saw little profit in going to the police.

Then she bought the new battery and aerial, and now was ready for their next move. She knew they were still scheming, and she sat and listened each night after Charlie had left for the pub. There had been a confusing discussion about touch-papers and fuses. Putting two and two together, she assumed that the discussion was linked in some way to Mill House, and that everything that was linked to Mill House, was linked in some way to Three Bridges.

Thinking back, she was reasonably sure that when the dog had escaped from the van that night, it had headed up through the gate and taken the track into the woods. Perhaps there was some way of getting to the house over the hill. She resolved to find out.

One afternoon, when Charlie was at work, she took the bicycle and a good pair of boots, and rode down the hill to Three Bridges. She opened the gate and pushed the bicycle up the muddy lane into the woods.

A vehicle had been there before her, and it wasn't a tractor. She could see that from the tyre marks in the mud. Although the mud was beginning to dry out, she could also see the prints of people and dogs, both coming and going. When she got to the first quarry, there was a well-defined track leading into it.

This might be it, she thought, something to do with what they were up to. She followed the track, through the thick layers of moss, and into the far corner. An unsuccessful attempt had been made to hide the prints with leaves and moss. In the corner of the quarry there was a thicket centred on a young oak. She pulled the vegetation aside and uncovered the entrance to a narrow cave.

She hadn't thought of that, and hadn't brought a torch with her either. So although she peered inside, and contemplated going further in, she decided against it. She replaced the vegetation and made her way home on the bicycle.

The following afternoon she found a torch and retraced her steps. She investigated the crevice and quickly discovered the boxes. They smelt decidedly strange and she decided not to push her luck by playing about with them too much.

The smell reminded her slightly of spent fireworks, which she guessed meant dynamite or something. At the far end of the crevice there was a plank wall, she knocked on it a few times but couldn't hear anything on the other side. She left the cave and stood in the quarry contemplating things for a while. The wooden wall had to be an entrance straight into Mill House itself.

That had to be why they were down there so frequently. They must be creeping in to the house when no one was looking. They were lucky that nobody had caught them at it. If that was their strategy, she had no intention of following them in. After all, she might be caught rather than them.

With her receiving equipment, she didn't really need to be near the place anyway. She just needed to know when they were going to do whatever it was they were planning. Then if she could trap the two recalcitrants in the cave – she might be able to get Charlie away.

That would do it, if she could get him out and them into the house at the same time. Then the police would pick them up and take them off to the nearest available jail cell. Then Charlie would come back home and do what he was supposed to do, like mend the fuses and put in a new kitchen. That would do the trick very nicely indeed, so all she needed to do was wait.

The next question was; when they did whatever they were planning, how was she going to get Charlie out and the other two back into the cave. She couldn't think of anything for a long time, but then it struck her there was one thing that would make them all do exactly as they were told. That was a shotgun. Charlie didn't have a shotgun, but she suspected that both Archie and Ivan had them. Ivan's place was probably quite difficult to get into, but Archie's, well that was a different matter, as the old man didn't even bother to lock his door.

There was only one problem with all of this and that was timing, the bicycle was just too slow. Once she knew the game was afoot, she would need to be quick, very quick.

The following evening she decided that she would have to buy a moped. It was the only way she was going to get around fast enough. She had no driving licence, but on a provisional she would be allowed to drive a little moped. She looked in the local paper, noted three adverts for mopeds and wrote the phone numbers down on a scrap of paper.

Then she complained to Charlie, "my legs are getting so tired going up and down all those hills on the bicycle, can't you get me something with a motor?" He complained about the money, but she knew it was just stinginess, and in the end he gave way. Anything for a peaceful life. She rang up the three sellers, and eventually chose a small Honda. She guessed that at 100cc it would probably be a little bit quieter than the other two. She didn't want to give the game away by making a blasted awful noise.

The following day Charlie took her to Lapford in the car and they bought the thing. And over the next few days she learnt to ride it, with Charlie pushing and giving instructions from the patio while she wobbled round the garden.

She then waited until he was at work before she experimented with silencing the thing. She used rags, which she tied around the exhaust pipe and found that by covering the end with some light filament and wrapping enough round it, she could quieten it quite a bit. It got a bit hot if she ran it for too long, but for short bursts it was quite safe.

About a week later, again sitting in her sewing room, she overheard the conversation in which they agreed that the Thursday evening at eleven o'clock was decided upon.

Chapter 29

Charlie would probably leave the house early in the evening, Maureen thought. She expected him to go and join the other good-for-nothings at Ivan's house. She hadn't overheard that part of the conversation, but since that had been what they'd done in the past; she guessed they'd do it again.

That Thursday evening Charlie left just after eight as she'd expected. She listened to the noise of the car disappearing into the distance. Then she put on her warm clothes, and took the mask and hat from their hiding place in the hall cupboard. She put them into the box on the back of the moped and rode down to Archie's house.

She hid the moped by the back door, and peered about her. The lights were out and everything was quiet. Across the valley an owl called, and in the distance she could hear the faint gurgle of the river, rushing on down toward the sea.

She tried the back door, and found it open. The old fool never bothered to lock anything! She let herself in and crept quietly round the house in the dark.

"Now where would the old idiot keep a shotgun?" she thought, as she searched through cupboards and under chairs. But it wasn't exactly very well hidden. She found it propped up in the kitchen cupboard along with assorted saddlery. The cartridge belt was hung on a hook beside it. She checked the gun wasn't loaded. Then took four cartridges from the belt, and stuffed them into her coat pocket. Leaving the house, she closed the door quietly behind her and strapped the shotgun to the back of the seat. She froze for a few seconds as a car went by in the road. Then she wheeled the moped back onto the tarmac and made her way to Three Bridges.

When she got there she opened the gate and let herself through. She pushed the moped up a few yards, and then returned to close the gate behind her. She then rode far enough up the lane so as not to be visible from either road or quarry. She secreted the moped behind a convenient holly bush, and settled down to wait.

Now it was then just a question of patience. She sat on a log and listened to a couple of owls calling to each other across the valley. Once a hedgehog came snuffling round her feet. It was a long wait, and quite spooky in the dark. For a while a soft drizzle fell through the branches above her. Then at about ten thirty she heard noises, chains rattling and the gate opening, then a vehicle being driven up toward her through the woods.

Three figures climbed out of the van, and she watched them through a screen of holly. They made their way up to the quarry and then straight into the cave in the far corner. She crept nearer and hid behind a tree. From inside the quarry she could hear mumbled conversation. The three men were discussing how to set the fuses off.

"We have to tie all the fuses together," explained Ivan, "then we light the taper, and we should have about three minutes." He did it with some expertise, even after twenty-eight years.

"And the gas grenades, they give you a couple of minutes at most." he explained.

Archie had gone down and opened the scullery door slightly. Then he pulled the cupboard back to within a few inches of the wall. Ivan and Charlie had meanwhile finished tying the fuses. When all three had returned and were ready, Ivan lit the fuse. Then they grabbed handfuls of smoke grenades and headed back to the mouth of the cave. That should be quite sufficient to clear the house out, and there were still several hundred left, which they could use if the need arose. They turned back at the last moment, pulled pins and threw their gas grenades into the depths of the cave.

They watched to see where the grenades landed, and backed out into the evening light. Just as they were pushing back through the thicket, suddenly and most unexpectedly a gruff voice from behind them shouted, "STAND STILL!" And they turned in surprise, and their blood froze. A figure behind them was pointing a shotgun directly at Ivan.

"What the Hell!" Ivan said, and the figure jabbed the gun alarmingly at him. The three men rapidly put their hands into the air and retreated back towards the cavern.

"Can't go in there!" whispered Archie.

They now perceived that the gruff figure sported a strange woolly cap and a particularly demented pig mask.

Suddenly the figure pointed the shotgun into the air and let off one of the cartridges. A thunderclap of an explosion buffeted their ears and boomed around the quarry. Then the gun was levelled at them again. There was no mistaking that whoever was behind the mask meant business.

"YOU TWO," shouted the voice, "BACK IN THE CAVE!"

Ivan and Archie were herded back towards the cavern.

"Christ" said Ivan, "We haven't got long, the whole bloody thing will blow."

"GET IN OR I SHOOT!" shouted the furious voice.

Charlie was then herded back out into the quarry. The gun was pointed at him briefly.

"RUN," he was told.

He didn't hesitate. Adrenaline gave him the legs of a much younger man, and fled into the night. The other two were forced back into the cavern.

"What the hell are we going t' do?" asked Archie.

Ivan was quicker; he was planning to put out the fuses. They couldn't stop the smoke grenades, but they might be able to extinguish the tear gas if they were fast enough. When he reached the crates it was too late. The fuse was gone, and tear gas had started to fizz. He felt his eyes beginning to smart. Only seconds later they were extremely sore.

"We've got to get back into the house!" shouted Archie.

"Hang on…" Ivan reached down for one of the smaller boxes they had brought from Trinity. He broke the lid off with a quick heave. Then with his eyes closed – against the pain - he groped around in the box for anything that might help them. He extracted a small handgun - standard issue military sidearm – he knew the feel even after all these years.

"Is it loaded?" asked Archie gasping. He still had an eye open even with the pain.

"No, but it should frighten him" replied Ivan.

They rushed back to the entrance, and Ivan peered tearfully through the vegetation that shrouded the mouth of the cavern. The pig-masked figure with the shotgun was still there. He held the gun out, two hand grip, and pointed it directly at him.

"PUT YOUR HANDS UP!" he shouted.

The figure was obviously extremely startled by this unexpected turnaround.

Maureen had been having difficulty seeing out of the tiny eyeholes in the mask as her glasses had misted up.

She turned; saw them; saw the gun, levelled the shotgun at them and pulled the trigger. There was a horrendous roar and the two men backed into the cave again. Archie received a couple of pellets in his shoulder and Ivan got one in his wrist. But Ivan was quick off the mark, and as soon as the noise had died down, Ivan moved. He advanced out of the cave with his gun pointed directly at the figure in the mask.

"RIGHT YOUR TURN," he shouted, "DROP THE GUN AND GET IN THE CAVE."

And the masked man did as he was told.

"IF YOU COME OUT, I WILL SHOOT YOU," Ivan shouted.

As the figure disappeared into the cave Archie looked at Ivan.

"Was that wise?" he asked.

"Not sure," admitted Ivan, "seems like the best policy."

Archie bent down and retrieved the abandoned shotgun.

Inside the cave Maureen, with a gun at her back, decided that the only safe course was to get through the house and out the other side as quickly as possible. She closed her eyes tightly, and with her arms in front of her, fled into the darkness.

En route she knocked against something, grazing her shin. What-ever-it-was fell to the floor at her feet, but she didn't stop. When she reached the wall at the far end, she hit it with enormous force and the cupboard collapsed in front of her. She tumbled over it into the scullery, and rolled into the centre of the room. In seconds she was up and into the house. It took her less than a minute, with smarting eyes and burning lips to find the front door. She unbolted it and was through and into the gardens before anybody realised she was there. She fled down the drive, tears streaming down her face, and her mouth and throat burning pepper hot. At least she was not to be intercepted by a security guard, a small mercy.

Back in the quarry the two figures followed in Charlie's footsteps as fast as they could.

"Get back to the van and let's get the hell out of here."

They shouted for Charlie when they reached the van and he appeared from behind a tree.

"What the hell happened?" he said.

"We turned the tables on him! Get in the van!" ordered Ivan.

They jumped in and with streaming eyes, Ivan drove slowly back towards Greenly as accurately as he could. As they drove into the yard, they heard a splinteringly loud explosion in the distance.

"What the hell was that!" exclaimed Archie.

"Buggered if I know, it can't have been us….. at least I don't think it was."

"Don't suppose those mortars have gone off do you?" asked Archie.

"Don't see how they could have!" replied Ivan.

Chapter 30

In her desperate haste to get out of the cave and into the house, Maureen had knocked the teargas over. They had fallen to the floor of the cave, where sparks from the fuses had by chance set light to a layer of dry wood under-laying the thin gravel.

This was the desiccated remains of the equipment that had been used, almost three hundred years before, to construct the quarry in the first place. It was made up of bits of wheelbarrow, planks, rope, blocks, wedges and fencing, and it proved great tinder.

Within minutes of Maureen's passage, a small but fierce fire was consuming the dry wood. In addition to the fumes from the grenades, large clouds of smoke issued from the burning floor, and began to leak into the scullery. Although the crates containing the rest of the equipment were still damp, they dried rapidly and joined in the conflagration.

Some minutes later, so did the first of the mortars. It exploded up with an astonishing boom that rocked the whole hillside, and set off two of the others. One of them flew straight out of the cave, through the quarry and into the river above Three Bridges. Another went in the opposite direction, straight through the scullery; the door, the far wall, the smoking room and out through the window into the garden. The noise of exploding incendiaries woke people three miles away in the village.

Upstairs, the occupants of Mill House were woken from brief sleeps by a series of horrendous explosions, and were thrown from their beds by violent shockwaves. They ran from their rooms and gathered, pyjama clad, on the landing. Peering around, dazed and confused, they tried to understand what the hell was going on. Thick smoke began billowing up the stairwell towards them.

"I think the house is on fire!" Richard said, stating the obvious, "let's get the hell out of here!"

They crept down the stairs hanging on to each other, and quickly discovered they could neither breathe nor see.

"Shit, my eyes hurt," said Mickel who was having some difficulty with the steps. The others tried to help, Richard led from the front and Shaun steadied him from behind. Eventually they reached the ground floor, but they could hardly breathe and their eyes were now clamped tight shut. A further series of loud explosions rocked the whole building and plaster fell from above.

"Got to get out of here quick," shouted one of the security guards between gasps, and with presence of mind led them through the front door and across drive. They stumbled out past the cars and collapsed on the lawns. Loud explosions continued and thick white smoke belched from every door and window. The security guards, in better condition than the others, pulled the musicians still further from the house.

"What in God's name's going on?" asked Richard.

"I'm damned if I know," replied a security guard.

One of them rushed off, blinking, in a car to phone the police.

Twenty minutes later the first fire engine arrived and started spraying water in through the windows. A fireman went in with breathing equipment and came out shortly after saying he could see little signs of fire but huge amounts of smoke.

Others followed him in but reappeared saying the smoke was coming from the kitchen area. Had they left a cooker on?

Then the fire crews on the hoses started having breathing difficulties, and spare masks had to be found. They said they couldn't see the windows, and had to be directed by shouts from behind. Tear gas was suspected.

Fortunately more engines arrived in the nick of time, and the Chief took control of the situation.

They went in with hatchets and breathing equipment to try and discover the source. From the far side of the lawn, the group and their minders watched with depressed curiosity. Once they had put out the small fires that had been started around the windows, the fire brigade traced the source of the smoke to the scullery at the rear of the building.

There were a series of forced retreats as more explosions took place in the house, and the Chief began to toy with the idea of calling either the bomb squad or the Porton Down chemical warfare unit.

Not being too sure about the cause, and with more of the ladder-men asking for breathing equipment after being almost blinded by the fumes, they decided that the best procedure would be to drench the scullery and hopefully the cause of the fire as quickly as possible.

They went in again with masks and oxygen, fighting their way through impenetrable fumes. After drenching the area with thousand of gallons of Torridge river water, they were amazed to discover the source of the blaze as being a cave at the rear of what had once been the scullery.

The senior officer went round taking statements and trying to discover how it had started. The whole thing was a complete mystery. None of them could understand what had happened. They knew nothing of any cave, and swore no cookers had been left on.

Inspector Carpenter had been called all the way from Bidstable, and was juggling feelings of irritation and curiosity. He talked with the fire chief and was told that there was no way that he would get a report until the following day. It would take that long to understand the cause of the incident, as they would have to wait for the smoke to clear.

"We can't get in there to see what's going on," he explained, "if we take our masks off, we suffer badly with the smoke, and with the masks on we can't see a bloody thing anyway!

Inspector Carpenter, fed up to the back teeth with Mill House, drove back to Bidstable in the squad car.

Chapter 31

For Joanna, things took a rather unexpected turn, as with Mill House out of action for the time being, the group had to find places in the village to stay. They had contemplated going to Exeter and finding a hotel, but the fire brigade said they should be able to get back into the house within a couple of days. So they had determined to stay locally, if at all possible.

Then Richard Fox turned up at The Royal Oak, hammering on the door. She leant out of an upstairs window to what was going on.

"Where's the fire?" she had asked.

"We need somewhere to stay," he explained.

"I'll be right down," she replied.

She opened up and let him in.

He explained that there had been a fire down at the house, which she knew, and they were trying to find accommodation for the group.

"I've got a couple of rooms you can have," she admitted, "one would probably suit you and there's another, but it's slightly smaller."

They discussed where the rest of the group might stay, and she made a number of suggestions. He disappeared to sort that out; reappearing later after the pub had opened.

So Richard moved into The Royal Oak, a most unexpected bonus. They had taken the rooms for three days, and she contemplated how she was to make him aware of the documentation she had on him.

There was no way she could simply give it to him. It was highly likely that he would turn nasty.

It could arrive in the post, but if she did post it, it might go via the sorting office in Exeter and arrive after he'd left.

Alternatively it could mysteriously appear on his bed, or be delivered by someone. The latter seemed the most sensible solution, after all. But if it just appeared on his bed, he would naturally wonder who had access to his room. No, an unknown courier seemed the best solution. She wondered who she could ask to do it. It had to be someone unknown in the village, as he was bound to ask questions. In the end she decided her cousin in North Molton would probably do, as not only was he unknown in Somleigh, but he owed her a favour anyway.

And yes, they definitely wanted to keep to themselves. More rooms were found elsewhere in the village, and things settled down once again.

The following day the police and the fire investigators made their report, and the bomb squad were called in. They turned up in dark green army vehicles and headed down through the village towards the house. This aroused no little discussion as to what else was going on down at Mill House.

"Those weren't police I saw, them was Army," one old woman told Joanna.

The next day she drove into Torrington. She made three photocopies of the file at the post office, and left the original and a copy with her solicitor in the Square. Then she bought a Hockings ice cream from the van on top of the hill, and then made her way home via North Molton.

That evening her cousin appeared in the bar while she was serving Ivan. He handed her an envelope, and left without saying a word. It was addressed to Richard Fox at Mill House. The typed address had been scratched out and the Royal Oak added in a scrawl to one side.

She gave it to her barmaid who took it up to Richard in his room.

Chapter 32

Someone knocked on Richard's door. He sat up, slipped the rather rude magazine he'd been reading under the bed, and perching on the edge said, "yes who is it?"

A voice on the landing said "There's a package here for you Mr Fox."

He stood up and went to the door, opened it and found one of the barmaids outside. She handed him a manila envelope, he grunted, and she disappeared back down the stairs. This was bound to happen; letters destined for the house would naturally be diverted to The Royal Oak.

He'd already spoken to the local post office, and had been assured that they would be diverted. He sat back down on the bed, and ripped the envelope open. Inside there appeared to be photocopies of official documents. He wondered who in hell was sending him things like this, and for a second thought it might be his accountant. But, then, suddenly, his blood froze ran cold, and the devil walked over his grave.

As he leafed through the pages, one after the other, his sense of shock became worse and worse. How in God's name anybody had got hold of this stuff, he couldn't begin to imagine. They were the sorts of documents he'd never wanted or expected to see. He wondered if he was having a nightmare, and tried to make himself wake up. He pinched his thigh to check, and it hurt.

Unfortunately he was defiantly awake.

He stared at the file, and wished he'd never seen it in the first place.

How in hell's name had somebody got hold of all this stuff, he had absolutely no idea. There were VAT reports in there, there ware Inland Revenue tax reports, there were receipts from the purchase of Mill House, and there was information about the purchase of the brewery, as well as the purchase of some of his other businesses. And he could see - without needing an accountant's brain - that many of the figures did not balance!

"Oh shit!" he said to himself, and repeated it again for good measure. He stared at the documents for a long time that evening, leafing through them, and wondering what in hell's name they were doing in his bedroom and what the hell he was going to do about it.

Well, this little lot would need to be destroyed and sharpish. There was a small fireplace in the room and although it didn't look like it had been used for a while, perhaps it would do. He found a box of matches next to the Bible in the draw of the bedside table, and started tearing the documents up. When he'd made a sufficient pile in the grate, he set fire to it.

Unfortunately, this didn't have the desired effect, mainly he realized too late, because the chimney had been blocked up. The smoke which should have gone up the flu, came straight back into the room instead. He rushed around opening windows and trying to get the smoke out by waving a magazine. After some minutes, someone in the street noticed smoke pouring from the window and rushed inside to inform Joanna that the pub was on fire. She ran upstairs accompanied by the bar maid, and hammered on the door. They tried the handle, but it was locked from the inside. Eventually he opened the door, and apologized.

"What's going on?" Joanna asked, "Is there a fire?"

"No," he lied, "um, I was just trying to keep warm, so I lit the fire."

"What, in the grate?"

"Yes."

"Well you can't do that," Joanna exclaimed, "the fire doesn't work - the chimney's blocked."

"Yes I know," he said.

Joanna sent the barmaid downstairs to find him a heater and together they put out the remains of the fire. He hid the remnants of the documents underneath the bed, and prevaricated his way out of a difficult situation.

That night he slept badly. Someone was trying to blackmail him - that was obvious - but what did they want out of him? Well, to his mind, that was obvious, it had to be money. But who had the intelligence and the contacts to gather all that material?

He knew the group couldn't, they simply didn't think like that. Whoever it was had to have his fingers in a lot of pies. Some of them were internal Inland Revenue documents, how in God's name had they got those. Maybe whoever it was worked for the Inland Revenue, or possibly for the Customs and Excise. Was it possible to work for both, he wasn't sure.

There wasn't much he could do - yet. His only option was to wait and see what the demands were. He sat on his bed the next day, and stared unseeing at the newspaper in front of him. He was waiting, and would continue to wait.

The following day the demands did arrive, but not quite in the manner he anticipated. He was expecting a letter, or possibly a phone call, but the blackmailer, took a slightly unusual route. At about three o'clock he got fed up with waiting and decided to dispose of the remaining official documents. He rolled them up with the newspaper and went out. He drove into the woods until he was some distance from the village, found a conveniently isolated spot and dug a hole and buried the papers. Nobody would ever find them in a place like that he thought.

When he got back to the car, wiping his hands with the leaves from a nearby tree, he was surprised to discover an envelope under the wipers. He pulled it out, leaving muddy fingerprints on the outside, and stared at the cover: 'R Fox' had been written in pencil on the front.

He looked around; expecting to see some figure hurrying away, but the lane and wood were silent and deserted. But at least he now had the demands, if that was what the envelope held. Whoever the blackmailer was, it had to be someone who knew his way around. After all, he'd not noticed anybody following him when he drove out of the village.

He decided not to open the envelope until he got back to his room. Anyway, he needed to wash his hands properly. He stuffed it into his pocket and drove back to the pub. He went straight up to his room, leaving muddy footprints on the carpet, washed his hands and then inspected the envelope.

Yes it was sealed tight, and they definitely knew his name. Well they would, wouldn't they, with all those documents. Whoever he was - he assumed it was a man – it must have taken months to get it all together.

He contemplated using the services of someone he knew in Southend - possibly to kneecap the bastard! That was an option he would very much like to use - if he got half a chance.

He tore the envelope open and pulled out a single typed sheet. It was very simple and said: 'the documents will be destroyed if you: 1. Sell all businesses acquired from Cordaxe, 2. Resign as manager of the Cordaxe and 3. Leave £10,000 in an envelope in the font of Somleigh Church.'

Chapter 33

And that was it. There was nothing more!

He couldn't work out what it was all about. The £10,000 he'd expected, but the rest of it was odd. Why resign from Cordaxe? He mulled this over and continued to worry about all night. It was the second night in a row that he'd slept badly.

His suspicions began to point back at members of Cordaxe. He'd known for a long time they'd wanted rid of him. But he had difficulties believing it was them, unless they'd hired someone. Just possibly they wanted rid of him more than he had expected. They knew a bit about the purchasing of the businesses from the Cordaxe, so they would have some information about his private affairs.

Perhaps they'd hired private investigators? No that couldn't be right he thought to himself, private investigators couldn't get their hands on internal documents from the Inland Revenue or Customs and Excise.

It was all very mysterious. It didn't tell him when to leave the money in the Church; it just said he was to leave it in the font. This was curious in itself, as he would have expected a time, or at least some further instructions. However, there was nothing like that at all, and to his mind it was decidedly strange. He sank gradually into a moody depression, and became increasingly unresponsive and sullen.

A couple of days later they were told that they could move back into the house. Richard moved with them, but with little enthusiasm. The rest of the household found him more bad tempered and miserable than ever, and kept a wide berth. He phoned a number of people in Southend for advice, as if he needed it. Then four days to the hour after having received the instructions, he told his solicitor in Basildon to begin selling the businesses.

"You should hold out for a better price," he was advised, "the market's a bit low at the moment. It would be better if you sold in the autumn - or even next year."

But Fox was adamant, "no, they have to be sold immediately, even if that means a loss."

It wasn't a big issue; after all he'd got them for next to nothing. He wasn't so sure however, about what to do with the money. If he'd been told when to leave the money, he could have had some heavies keeping watch, and break the legs of anybody who tried to collect it.

When he went to inspect the font, he found the Church locked. So the drop would have to take place when the church was open. Well of course it will be open on a Sunday he assumed.

That explained it, whoever was blackmailing him, expected him to leave the envelope sometime after the service on a Sunday. He phoned his friends in Southend again, and told them to come down. They were big lads and he agreed to pay them well. All they had to do was to keep an eye out for anybody interfering with the font during and after the service.

They came down by train via Tiverton early that Sunday morning. Later he put them back on the train, and paid them in fivers. He also offered them a bonus if they caught the sod, and they promised to return the following weekend. There had been no sign of anybody trying to open the font, or even looking at it. No one went near the thing. He decided that the following week, he would put an empty envelope in the font and see what happened. Perhaps somebody would go looking, and they could have a little fun.

Chapter 34

Inspector Carpenter was being antagonized, even more than usual. This latest one had been sent to try his patience. He was sure of it. An officer from the bomb squad had come to see him two days after the fire. And had informed him that the fire had been caused by military incendiaries.

This had rather surprised him; he'd assumed that the idiots had set fire to their own house by smoking marijuana or something equally stupid. The Major had however explained the presence of the cave behind the scullery, and had described how it went right through the hill. He had added that it was half full of military incendiaries of various forms.

"Mostly of a type used in the last war," he explained.

"Who set them off?" was what Carpenter wanted to know, but the Major was cagey on this point.

"We don't think they were set off in the conventional manner," he explained, "they appear to have been set off by a fire."

"And the fire?" asked Carpenter.

"The fire brigade told me," explained the Major, "that it may have been started deliberately."

"Why did they say that?" asked Carpenter.

"They can't find anything else that would have set it off," he explained, "no wiring or electrical supply in that area. In fact there's very little wiring in the scullery at all and certainly no electrical equipment within the cavern itself. So in the absence of an adequate explanation, they're opting for a malicious cause."

Carpenter thanked the Major, who left him his report and went back out to his MOD Land Rover. He'd need to see the Chief Constable, as he wasn't entirely sure what to do about this. So there was no indication as to who'd set the thing off, but it sounded like somebody had. Was it one of the idiots in the house? That was quite possible, but there was no evidence to support it. So he couldn't arrest anybody.

There didn't seem to be very much he could do. He wondered if he could put the scares on them. Perhaps if he pulled one of them in and put a bit of pressure on him, it was just possible he might open up and admit the truth. He went through the file again; he could see that they had had a pretty nasty time over the last few months what with one thing and another. The security guards will probably be quite tight lipped and difficult to break. The members of the group, well they had a lot to lose so probably wouldn't want to admit anything if they could possibly avoid it. But there was this business manager chap, he might talk. He next racked his brains for an adequate reason to arrest the man. He wondered what they had on him. He sent for the Sergeant, who appeared in his office some minutes later.

"Yes Sir."

"Have we got anything on the Cordaxe's business manager?"

"Criminal record?"

"Yes, I'd like to have a chat with him."

"I had a look last week Sir, but apart from speeding and other minor stuff, nothing. We could go down there and talk to him, but he might take offence at being arrested."

"Alright let's do that," said the inspector eventually.

So they took a squad car and headed for Mill House. They arrived an hour later, and knocked on the door. The windows were still boarded up, and many displayed burnt frames. Workmen were about, continuing the landscaping of the drive area. And builders were coming in and out with scaffolding.

They knocked and explained they wanted to talk to Richard Fox. A couple of minutes later he appeared on the doorstep.

"I'm Fox," he said.

They introduced themselves and were taken through into the study. Fox contemplated phoning a solicitor, but since he wasn't being arrested, he decided that it was no point in arousing their curiosity more than necessary. When all three men were seated, and the door was closed, the inspector began the interview.

"Do you have any reason to suspect the fire might have been started deliberately?" was his opening gambit.

"No," said Fox, "I assumed it was an electrical fault or something like that."

"Apparently not Mr. Fox," replied the inspector, "the Bomb Squad and the Fire Brigade tell us the cause was deliberate."

Fox looked surprised.

"I didn't know that," he said, "I was sure it was something to do with the wiring in the scullery or the kitchens or something.

"No" explained the inspector, "it was definitely deliberate. Can you think of anyone who might have a reason to plant high explosives in the house?"

"High explosives! Christ No! But I can think of a few people who don't like us much," Fox explained, "but I can't think of any who would want to kill us."

"So who would you regard as not liking you much then Mr. Fox?" asked the inspector.

"Well," he explained, "a few of the people who were hurt in the mudslide don't like us much. Oh and possibly some of our competitors as well. And there are a few people in the industry who don't see eye to eye with Mickel."

"Perhaps you could be a little more specific?" asked Carpenter.

And so the Sergeant made notes, while Fox spilled out a series of names.

"I can't think of anybody else," he said finally.

"All in all, you've had quite an interesting time here over the last few months haven't you Mr. Fox?" stated the inspector.

"That's true. Do you think there's a connection?" asked Fox.

"Well, first you have a catastrophic mudslide, then your musicians throw themselves out of windows and now this."

"The mudslide was something to do with the river. It wasn't deliberate, was it?" replied Fox.

"Actually," disagreed the inspector, "we think it was!"

That was news to Fox and surprised him quite considerably. His mind began to churn with thoughts that tied together mudslides, fires and blackmail. Someone was definitely out to get him. He wondered, briefly, if he could get any help from the inspector, but immediately rejected this.

In the end, the interview got virtually nowhere. It had worried the hell out of Fox, as the inspector had hoped, but for an entirely different reason.

When they got back in the squad car, the Sergeant said, "You frightened him alright."

But the inspector wasn't quite so sure.

"Yes," he said, "but he was hiding something."

They drove back to Bidstable discussing the causes of the mudslide and the fire at some length. The sergeant was firmly of the opinion that it was the same person that had caused both.

"Yes, but why?" asked the inspector. "If we had a motive, we would have some clue as to who's giving them such a hard time."

The sergeant thought it was the normal motive… money.

"There're a very successful band Sir, and they make vast sums of money. Maybe their competitors just want to sell more records. And are quite happy to do them a bit of damage to achieve this."

The inspector decided to find out if there were any new faces in the village. When they got back to Bidstable he told the Sergeant to go and ask a few questions.

"You never know," he said, "we might be lucky enough to catch them."

The following afternoon the Sergeant did as he'd been told and asked Helen lots of difficult questions about unknown faces in the village. She couldn't think of many.

"Yes there's lots of builders coming and going," she agreed. "And Mrs Rouse in the shop has seen quite a few people coming and going, oh and there were a couple of strange men in the church on Sunday."

"Oh yes what did they look like?"

"Oh big chaps," she said, "With muscles, you know kind of like bodybuilders or something."

"Did they say where they were from?" he asked.

"No, didn't say anything to anybody," she admitted, "funny thing was, they just sat there sullen like, through the service. Kept glaring at the font, very strange, didn't even sing the hymns!" she admitted.

Later the inspector decided that he would like to interview these two heavies, and made a mental note to have a word with them if they turned up on Sunday.

Chapter 35

Three weeks after the instruction had been received; the Bakery in Chulmleigh was sold. It didn't fetch the price Richard had wanted. That left three other businesses, and the brewery. He advertised them in local papers in Exeter, Bidstable and Okehampton, or at least his solicitor did. There was very limited interest in the brewery, and it occurred to him that it might be a problem. It was basically bankrupt, because not only had he run things down, intending to re-launch it for the London market, but it had sold very little to the local market recently. The books would have to be fixed first of course.

But in the end a buyer for the brewery appeared, accepting the modifications to the books readily. Richard got what he considered to be a reasonable price in the end. He'd been hoping for more, but was secretly relieved to be shot of it. It had been a bloody nuisance, and he was pleased it was all done and dusted at last. The other businesses followed suit some weeks later.

His friends from Southend came down each weekend, and sat in the Church watching the font. But no one ever went near the thing. Then the Police took an interest, but although suspicious, they had no reasons to detain them. However being stopped by the police on the way out of Church did little for their anonymity.

All the businesses sold in the end. His Solicitor told him that the purchasers were mainly local businesses trying to expand chains. Ferrets had been interesting, because it was bought a by a solicitor presumably working for an anonymous client. His nose told him something was queer about that, and of course he tried to find out who the purchaser was, but with no success. Had the blackmailer been after one of the businesses? Was that what it was all about? He couldn't see sense in that at all, they were all small, and the brewery was failing and would probably be bankrupt soon. Even if it didn't, it would trundle along making very little money, so he couldn't imagine anybody going to all that trouble for nothing.

Then he'd begun to wonder about his old business partner, and had the heavies ask him a few questions. But it appeared that he had completely new interests and denied strongly that he had anything to do with either Cordaxe or Devon. And as the two heavies had been sitting on him at the time Richard felt that he could probably believe this.

The members of the group had continued to needle him about the businesses, and to take the mickey in their normal way. It made him wonder, if after all if it was them that were blackmailing him. Would they set fire to their own house? And what about the explosives? That seemed a bit extreme even for them. He wasn't sure, but was beginning to think that he ought to cast his net a bit wider. After all if it wasn't his ex-business partner, and it wasn't anyone within the

Cordaxe, perhaps it was a competitor. Or perhaps it was nobody he knew at all. After all, maybe the selling of the businesses and resigning from the Cordaxe was just a front, to confuse him, a red herring. Maybe the whole thing was the £10,000, and that was it there was nothing else to it, and the other factors were purely meant to cast his suspicions astray.

In the end, he realized that he didn't have much choice. A second package had arrived, identical to the first, and this time there had been a covering note with it, it had merely said "half way." That he understood, and presumed it meant that he was half way through the instructions. As before he drove into the countryside, watching his rear view mirror this time, found a convenient spot and buried the offending documents.

One afternoon he drove up to the Royal Oak, and asked Joanna if she happened to know if the church was open any other time during the week.

"Are you getting religious?" asked Joanna.

"Oh I just wanted to have a look round," he feigned an interest in religious history.

"I don't think so," she said, "I think it's mainly Sundays, they had some stuff pinched a few years ago. If you want to look around you'll have to ask the Vicar, but I'm sure he'll let you in any time."

"Oh," he said, "thanks."

The following afternoon, after a long internal debate, he submitted his resignation in writing to Mickel. He walked into the drawing room, put the envelope down next to Mick's drink and walked straight out again. Mickel had looked at it suspiciously, before opening it, but when he did was astonished by its contents.

"Look at this," and he passed the note to Shaun.

They were stupefied as he was.

"I didn't think we'd ever get rid of him," said Mickel later, "but why does he resign now?"

"Why does he ever do anything?" said Shaun, "money, it's got to be something to do with money, it always is. Perhaps he's got a better job, or a better offer. It's better not to ask. He'd never tell us anyway."

Later Mickel sat down at the typewriter in his bedroom and composed a reply. To be sure he didn't claim for unfair dismissal he said what a good employee he'd been and thanked him for his service and said 'yes they would accept his resignation'. He slipped the letter into an envelope and stuck it on Fox's pillow. Fox left the following day. He went back to the Royal Oak for a couple of days, and wandered up to the church to see if was open.

On the Friday he went to the bank in Exeter, and returned with a large envelope.

On the Sunday he went to Church, and sat through the service with the two heavies. Afterwards he made his way to the back of the Church and placed the envelope in the center of the stone cavity.

He then closed it and joined the heavies in the porch. They waited until the Vicar had locked the Church. No one had gone anywhere near the font or shown any interest in it. They sat in the car and watched the Church all that evening. Parting with such a large sum of money was a painful experience. Later he returned to the Royal Oak and began a vigil of the Church. The two heavies got a taxi back to their train at Tiverton. Then he sat on the bed and watched the Church through his bedroom window. But he had to sleep, and couldn't watch every minute of every day. In his heart of hearts he knew he would never see the envelope again.

If ever he found out who the hell had been blackmailing him, he decided that he would kill the bastard. Breaking legs and kneecaps was pure generosity as far as he was concerned. But he had no option, if he wanted those documents shredded and destroyed - he had to do what the blackmailer demanded. But he had years, he would wait, and watch and eventually he'd get the bastard.

He still had plenty of money, and was convinced that sooner or later someone would put him on to the blackmailer. "If it takes me fifty bloody years," he said to himself, "I'll get the bastard. He'll be pushing up daisies well before I am."

Chapter 36

The following Friday, the Vicar went in to prepare for the Christening on the Saturday morning. He checked the flowers and added the parent's choice of hymns to the board. Later he ran through a rehearsal with Sunday's 3 o'clock wedding party.

His last task before locking the Church was to refill the font. He filled a jug from the vestry tap, and took it through, before heaving the lid off the font. He placed this, with some difficulty on a convenient pew. Then he took the jug of water, intending to fill the bowl in the base of the font.

But he was very surprised to find a large manila envelope in the bowl! He balanced the jug on one side, extracted the envelope and poured the water into the bowl. After replacing the lid he inspected the envelope. There was nothing written on the outside, but it contained something bulky, he thought it might be a book - perhaps a prayer book. But why would anybody want to put a prayer book in the font he couldn't imagine. Well, he judged that as there was no name on the envelope, he would have to open the thing and see what was in it.

He had to sit down. The shock of it! There were piles and piles of money, and he couldn't believe his eyes. There were fifty pound notes in there; in fact it was almost all fifty pounds notes. He flicked through it; it was wrapped in elastic bands, and what appeared to be official bank folders to hold it in place. Somebody had left it for the Church repairs!

It wasn't a normal way of making a donation at all; in fact it was extremely abnormal, it was all very odd. Possibly the donor must have wanted to remain

115

anonymous.

He was flabbergasted. He sat there for another ten minutes staring at the money before deciding what to do. Well there was only one thing he could do and that was to take it straight to the bank. He put it into the inner pockets of his cassock. In fact he had to split it and it filled all the pockets in both cassock and trousers. The he walked back to the house in a dreadful hurry, locking the Church door behind him.

He got the paying-in book from his study, and saying nothing to his wife who looked at him with some consternation, he jumped into the car and headed for Lloyds in Torrington. An hour later the money was safely deposited under lock and key in the Church's account. There had been much conversation and great surprise from the bank manager and his staff, who were as amazed by the sudden windfall as he'd been. In all his many years, he'd never had such a moment. They counted it in a machine that flicked through the notes, and he was able to see the total, £9,825, quite extraordinary.

He drove back to the village, but instead of going home, he let himself into the Church, and locked the door. He went and knelt in front of the altar and spent twenty minutes in prayer.

It was a wonderful moment; he would never forget it as long as he lived. He went home and told his wife all about it and she was as incredulous and pleased as he was. He was so ecstatic that he caught her in his arms and waltzed her round the hall. It was a wonderful moment.

He had wanted to tell everybody, it was just too much to bear. He wouldn't be breaking any confidences, because he'd no idea who the donor was. For a while he sat and stared at the television, but in the end it got the better of him. He put his coat on and headed for the pub, he was like a little boy with a new toy.

He let himself into the bar with an enormous smile, and told Joanna, and Archie and Ivan and many others.

And his happiness was unbridled. And they were all very pleased for him. They asked him how much it was and he told them almost ten thousand pounds. They were staggered; such a sum of money was unheard of in the village.

"So that'll get the bells mended?" asked Ivan.

"Absolutely and there will be ample left over to help the Parish," he confirmed. Later after they'd bought him a drink, Joanna came over to the table where the four men were sitting. Archie was there with his pipe; clouds of smoke billowing up above his head. Ivan was there as usual with his great ears, red face and baldhead, and Charlie having forgotten to remove his green hat.

"Gentlemen," she said, "I'd like to buy you a round."

"Well that's kind of you," said Ivan, and the others nodded their thanks.

"Charlie come up to the bar will you," she said, "and help me with this one." Ivan and Archie exchanged glances.

When Charlie reappeared it was not, as they had expected with more toxic bloody cider, but with beer.

"What's this?" asked Archie suspiciously.

"It looks like Ferrets!" said Charlie.

"Can't be," said Ivan, "she wouldn't dare, not after last time."

They looked enquiringly at Charlie who shrugged his shoulders. He placed Five pints of Ferrets on the table with some ceremony. They then sat down, and Joanna joined them.

"Gents," she said formally, "here's to Ferrets, and to Jim Lemon."

Eyebrows were raised.

"Come on then," she said, "try it!"

Five pints of Ferrets were solemnly raised to cautious mouths. As the fluid swirled around inside their mouths, they were staggered, and surprised, and delighted - it was the real stuff again!

The mood changed and the pints were sunk in single draught. Only the Vicar and Joanna took their time. And there was great merriment and laughter in the pub that evening.

"How did you do it?" they asked Joanna, when they eventually got their breath back. But she tapped the side of her nose and remained silent. Later, after she had returned to the bar to serve a carpenter from Dowford, Ivan went and joined her.

"Go on then," he said, "tell all."

"I bought the brewery," she said.

"You what!" he said - astonished.

"Yes, it was for sale, so I bought it."

Tears streamed down his face as the laughter came, "I don't believe it," he said, "wait till I tell the others about this."

"No," she stopped him, "It's just our little secret, just keep it under your hat for the time being will you?"

"Why's that?" he asked, surprised.

"I don't want Richard Fox to know it was me," she explained.

"Ah," he said, "well it was a wonderful thing you did Joanna, a really wonderful thing,"

But she shrugged her shoulders, "It makes good business sense you see," she explained, "I wasn't selling any beer, and now I will be!"

He took his handkerchief out and rubbed the tears from his face.

"You really did do a great thing Joanna, thank you so much."

Chapter 37

Maureen hadn't been herself for some time. She hadn't been nearly as irritable as normal, and had cooked his supper every evening, which had surprised the hell out of him. He had been getting used to living on a diet of takeaways, but here she was, cooking for him, mending his clothes and doing all the little things that a wife is supposed to do.

"You seem in a good mood these days," he commented.

"Oh, just getting used to the place," she said coyly.

That night, four weeks before, after she'd made her escape through Mill House, she'd taken a long time getting home. Mainly because that dreadful stuff in the cave had almost completely blinded her. So although she'd made it through the house and on to the road, things had not become any easier for Maureen.

She had then had an extremely unpleasant time, as not only could she not see at all well, but she was having difficulty breathing as well. She had eventually collapsed in the road, and was taken by ambulance to Bidstable Hospital. There, a junior doctor, assuming she was having a serious asthma attack had injected her with steroids and aminophyllin. Then, to make things even more unpleasant, he nebulised her with salbutamol. Then realizing his error, he had proceeded to wash her eyes with a sodium chloride solution.

The whole procedure was overseen by a large burley nurse, who could have made a better living castrating pigs. She was later sent home in another ambulance, having experienced more pain and discomfort than she could possibly have imagined. She stumbled into the house still in shock. It had been worse than the nights she had spent watching Greenly Barton, far worse.

She had crept up to her bedroom without waking Charlie, and slept badly. Although she'd been late home that night, Charlie never mentioned it. Mainly she assumed, as the ambulance which had brought her home had refrained from using it's siren on the way through the village!

But now Charlie was in a better mood, and so she had decided that Ivan could go and bury his head in the sand. She was not going to spend her life following him around, trying to get him arrested and jailed. He could do perfectly well on his own. In the meantime, she had decided to make the best of a bad job, and so had reverted to being the good little housewife she had been years before.

At first it rankled a tiny bit, but soon she found that some satisfaction came with it, which rather surprised her. And she gradually discovered that as she was nicer to him, he was nicer back. And as he was nicer to her she found herself being more pleasant to the locals.

Perhaps she could make a go of it after all! She hid the bugs and receiving equipment in a box in the attic. The moped proved a great boon, and she found she liked the new freedom. One afternoon she went to Torrington and did some shopping. On another occasion she went down to Crediton. It really did give her liberty to get about. Life wasn't so bad, it was warm, and the sun was bright, and people were cheerful.

One day her cousin came to visit her from Coventry, and stayed for a whole week. And Maureen became quite chummy with one of the ladies in the hairdressers. And asked if she could get a job there and was accepted. After all she had done it years before, and although things had changed a little bit, they weren't that different. Life was going to be better now she was sure of it and somehow as the weeks passed she forgot all about Ivan.

Chapter 38

Archie was on his way to check his traps. He'd put them down the previous night and had used wire snares as per usual. He was hoping to get three or four rabbits that day, which he'd be able to sell to the butcher. He made a little out of this to supplement his meager pension.

Followed the rhododendron hedge bordering the gardens of Mill House, he recovered the snares one by one. It was a good day and he got six rabbits. He put them into a bag, slung it over his shoulder and started back. He planned to take them up to the butcher and swap for some really good baccy. Since he was there however, he decided to have a peer through the hedge and see what he could see going on at Mill House.

When he stuck his nose into the hedge, he was astonished to discover that someone had got there before him. There was a man in there, sitting on a branch. He had a camera on a tripod pointed at the house.

"Hello!" said Archie surprised.

The photographer looked at him at first with some hostility, but then seeing that he was certainly not a photographer and didn't look anything like any member of the press he'd ever seen, he gave him a grin.

"What's up?" he said.

"What you doing here?" asked Archie.

"Pictures," the man said stating the obvious.

"Are you trying to get some photographs of those men, the Cordaxe?" Archie asked him.

"That's right," he said.

Archie told him about the point on top of the hill where he'd sat and watched the house.

"That's quite a good spot," he said, "you can see in the back windows from there."

The photographer thanked him and Archie made his way to the butcher with his rabbits.

Later that evening he saw Ivan in the pub. Ivan told him that his housekeeper had told him that the shopkeeper, who was her cousin, had had people asking where the Cordaxe were based. They'd popped into the shop that lunchtime and she'd sent them down towards Mill House.

'They didn't look like the normal builders,' his housekeeper had told him. 'They looked different somehow, smarter, but sort of roguish,' was what the shopkeeper had told her.

"They must have been photographers," said Archie, "I bumped into one in a hedge."

"Ah!" said Ivan, "I don't suppose they'll like that much down at Mill House. Remember Fox told the Vicar that they came down here for the peace and quiet. If they get a load of photographers taking snaps they aren't going to like it much."

There were more new faces seen in the village over the next few days. They went into the shop asking for the Cordaxe, and one even came into The Royal Oak, and. All was sent obligingly down to Mill House.

Charlie told the other two that evening, "They're all over the place, lenses pointing out of every bush in sight. I can't mow the grass without them taking photographs of me."

Three days later the Cordaxe left. A cortege of Rolls Royce's and Mercedes, packed with hangers-on and members of the group disappeared up the drive from Mill House. They drove through Somleigh and disappeared down the road towards Tiverton. It was the last any of them ever saw of the Cordaxe.

In time the house was sold, and a retired solicitor from Bristol bought it.

And in time, the Cordaxe, were forgotten, as was Richard Fox.

And things went back to much the way they'd always been. The Royal Oak was as it had always been, for the locals, for proper Devonians. Trades people went to The Union, and the new arrivals from the housing estate went to the George and listened to juke boxes.

In time everything settled down again just the way it had been. About six months after the Cordaxe had left, Joanna went shopping in Taunton one Saturday afternoon. In her handbag she had a newspaper cutting. At least it looked like a newspaper cutting, or a photocopy of a newspaper cutting. Actually a typesetter in Ledbury had created it for her at some cost.

It said: 'Cassandra de Filias had died tragically on Monday afternoon on the island of Rhodes, when the car she was traveling in was hit by a lorry containing thirty-five tons of ready mix concrete'. There was even a blurred photograph. She went to the flat and stuck the photograph onto the flat's street door. A sad end to an era, but thus died Cassandra de Filias.

In offices and houses around the southwest, ex-public schoolboys grieved. In Bristol, a high-up in the offices of Her Majesties Inspectorate of Customs and Excise grieved worse of all. His tribute to her was to extract the little file he'd produced so many months before, and send it with his compliments to the Inland Revenue.

Richard Fox was to be his tribute to Cassandra. The man would share his grief. Cassandra must have had a reason for not liking the chap, which must have been why she'd asked for the file. So even in death, she would have her revenge on the man, for whatever injustice he'd committed against her.

A year and a half later, Richard Fox, then running a pornographic bookshop and living in Westcliffe-on-Sea, was found guilty on eighteen counts of fraud, tax evasion and larceny, and was imprisoned for a period of twenty-two years.

He was also bankrupted.

www.ingramcontent.com/pod-product-compliance
Lightning Source LLC
Chambersburg PA
CBHW070342130626
46556CB00007B/2993